BENIGNA
MACHIAVELLI

Charlotte Perkins Gilman

BANDANNA BOOKS   1994   SANTA BARBARA

INTRODUCTION copyright © 1993 Bandanna Books
BENIGNA MACHIAVELLI was originally published serially in *The Forerunner,* edited by Charlotte Perkins Gilman.

Cover design: Joan Blake
Cover photo of Charlotte Perkins Gilman at age 24 was taken in 1884 by Elliott & Fry, a London studio; reproduced courtesy of the Schlesinger Library, Radcliffe College
Text design: Words Worth of Santa Barbara

ISBN 0-942208-18-8   LC 93-072625

ॐ   # INTRODUCTION

Benigna Machiavelli has never before been published in its entirety in book form. It was first published by Charlotte Perkins Gilman in *The Forerunner* (Vol. 5, 1914), a magazine which she wrote, edited, and produced every month from 1906 to 1916. The novella was serialized a chapter an issue. *The Forerunner* cost $1.00 per issue, and was in a 7″ x 10″, 28-page format. The circulation averaged 1,500 subscribers a year, including many in Europe, also some in India and Australia.

Gilman stated she did not "aim in the least at literary virtuosity," she was interested in ideas. The main idea expressed in *Benigna* is the story of a benign Machiavellian girl/woman, a "good villain," as Benigna phrases it. Having noted in the stories she read as a child that the villains exerted their intellects to accomplish their goals, while the heroes were "mostly very stupid" and practiced passive virtues, Benigna decides to apply her precocious mind to become this "good villain"—all for everyone's good, of course, at least as Benigna sees it. She responds to the sometimes onerous and perplexing life circumstances she observes herself to be in by deciding to take control of her life in highly creative (and manipulative) ways— at a time when women, and especially children, had very little control.

Benigna is an intensely insightful child, as was no doubt Gilman herself. How much of this story is based on her own life experiences is difficult to say; however there are many similarities. In her autobiography, *The Living of Charlotte Perkins Gilman,* she recounts the anecdote of the experiment to see what would happen if she broke the oppressive silence of her schoolroom, just as Benigna does (and with the same results). It's likely that much of Benigna's character is based on her own, doubtless with some amount of wishful thinking that she had as successfully taken as much control of her own life.

The family portrayed bears little resemblance to Gilman's, with the exception of the mother. Gilman had one sibling, a brother, Thomas A. Perkins, 14 months her senior, with whom she was not close. Her father, Frederick Beecher Perkins, left the family when Gilman was an infant and was infrequently in contact with them. However, her mother, Mary Wescott Perkins, described by Gilman as "absolutely loyal, as loving as a spaniel which no ill treatment can alienate," accurately describes Benigna's mother as well. Also similarly, Mary Wescott Perkins was intensely interested in "child culture," and had studied the Kindergarten method of child raising.

Another direct parallel to Gilman's life is Benigna's happily-ever-after ending, her marriage to her cousin. Gilman married her first cousin, George Houghton Gilman, seven years her junior. Unlike Benigna, this was her second marriage and, by her account, finally a happy one. In her autobiography she wrote, "we were married . . . and lived happily ever after. If this were a novel, now, here's the happy ending."

A word about the editing—True to the style of the day, Gilman's language tended at times to the dramatic, which often appears melodramatic to a modern reader. Numerous exclamation marks were omitted in the interest of giving emphasis where it was needed. An overly "cute" portrayal of the child Benigna's speech was toned down, and here and there "Oh!"s were deleted, again in the interest of retaining the drama without using melodrama. The generic "he" has been replaced with non-sexist usage. Benigna and/or Gilman's occasional sexist remarks about "boys" were toned down where it was possible, although at times they interfered with the story too much to be gracefully edited, and perhaps such remarks are useful to reveal the character, or the author.

Charlotte Perkins Gilman at 40, photo by Pearl Grace Loehr, reproduced courtesy of the Schlesinger Library, Radcliffe College

Although at present best known for her short story "The Yellow Wallpaper," a fictionalized account of her devastating first marriage, in her time Charlotte Perkins Gilman was known internationally as a lecturer and author of *Women and Economics: The Economic Relation Between Men and Women as a Factor in Social Evolution,* first published in 1898 by Putnam. A second printing followed in 1899, a third in 1900, a fourth in 1905 (by G.P. Putnam's Sons in London), a fifth in 1908, a seventh in 1912, an eighth in 1915, and a ninth in 1920. Given this kind of publishing history, it is amazing that her reputation has sunk to such obscurity, even taking into consideration the lack of interest in women's rights and other progressive ideas that followed the First World War.

Charlotte Perkins Gilman was born Charlotte Anna Perkins on July 3, 1860, in Hartford, Connecticut. She died on August 17, 1935, in Pasadena, California. Her death was a suicide by chloroform, a decision she made as a result of a breast cancer diagnosed as fatal. In an article regarding suicide she had written that it was "an insult to allow death in pitiful degradation." As in so many things, Gilman was ahead of her time in her views on euthanasia. Although this particular article was written knowing she was going to take her life, she had addressed the subject of suicide long before.

Lyman Beecher was her great grandfather on her paternal side, and she was influenced by this remarkable family's progressive ideas and attitudes. When her father, Frederick Beecher Perkins, left his family with little to no financial support, her mother, Mary Fitch Wescott Perkins, had few alternatives; she needed to rely on the charity of relatives, which included the Beechers. As a child, Gilman was visited by her great aunts Harriet Beecher Stowe and Catharine Beecher, the latter widely known in America at the time for having defined "a new role for women within the household."

Gilman was sought out and respected by George Bernard Shaw, who asked her to read *Candide* and give him her opinion. William Dean Howells said of her: "The best brains and best profile of any woman in America." The New York Fabians spoke of her as "a worthy female counterpart of G. B. Shaw." When H. G. Wells came to the United States in 1904, she was the one person he asked to meet. Theodore Dreiser also asked to meet her.

Her magazine was well-named. As a particularly acute, clear-sighted, articulate social reformer and feminist, she was one of the outstanding forerunners of our own time, and much can still be learned from her ideas.

Joan Blake
September 1993

BENIGNA
MACHIAVELLI

CHAPTER ONE

When I was a very young girl I heard a New Year's Prayer given by our minister, the Rev. William V. Cutter, a liberal and a learned man, with a great command of language. He was sort of intoning, as people do in prayer. And, by the way, how do Christian ministers reconcile it with their consciences to pray so when the Bible distinctly forbids us to make long prayers in public?

But they do make them, and this one went droning along with "Thou knowest" this, and "Thou knowest" that, to fill in. It used to puzzle me a good deal, these "Thou knowests." I was always taught it was vulgar to say "you know" all the time in conversation, and I couldn't see why it was any better in King James's English than Queen Victoria's.

"Thou knowest, O Lord," he went on in a sort of chant, "how many good resolutions we made a year ago today, and how we have broken them all; how many noble determinations we recorded, and how utterly we have failed to keep them."

It was all I could do to sit still in the pew. I wanted to

get up and tell that worthy man that there was one person at least in his church who had made good resolutions a year ago that day and kept them—every one. There weren't but three. The year before there were only two. And the year before that only one. That's the way to keep good resolutions—be economical with them.

People don't seem to use any judgment about their resolutions. They aspire by jerks to all sorts of perfection, make a jump for it, miss it, and then complain of the futility of human effort. Just look at the personal revelation books, those people who wail to us from Paris and St. Petersburg and Butte, Montana, always fussing and lamenting and blaming Providence or Fate or something. The utmost of their effort seems to be to arouse the sympathy of a listening world in their melancholy failures. I should think they would be ashamed. Why don't they *do* things? Look at Jean Valjean—when he was a convict, a poor, crushed, helpless prisoner—he set to work and learned wonderful gymnastic tricks—how to crawl up in the corner of a room by pushing against the wall, and things like that. There is always something you can do if you are any good.

I learned a lot, when I was a child, from novels and stories, even fairy stories have some point to them—the good ones. The thing that impressed me most forcibly was this: the villains always went to work with their brains and accomplished something. To be sure they were "foiled" in the end, but that was by some special interposition of Providence, not by any equal exertion of intellect on the part of the good people. The heroes and middle ones were mostly very stupid. If bad things happened, they practised patience, endurance, resignation, and similar virtues; if good things happened they practised modesty and magnanimity and virtues like that, but it never seemed to occur to any of them to make things move their way. Whatever the villains planned for them to do, they did, like sheep. The same old combinations of circumstances would be worked off on them in book after book—and they always tumbled.

It used to worry me as a discord worries a musician. Hadn't they ever read anything? Couldn't they learn anything from what they read—ever? It appeared not.

And it seemed to me, even as a very little child, that what we wanted was good people with brains, not just negative, passive, good people, but positive, active ones, who gave their minds to it.

"A *good* villain. That's what we need!" I said to myself. "Why don't they write about them? Aren't there any?"

I never found any in all my beloved story books, or in real life. And gradually, I made up my mind to be one.

My sister Peggy was over a year older than I. She was a dear, good child, and people liked her. They liked her before they liked me, because she was so pretty. And I saw that because so many people liked Peggy they did nice things for her, so I made up my mind to be liked too. I couldn't be as pretty, but then people like other things; it wasn't hard to find out how to please them.

At first I got into trouble more than Peggy did, from being more enterprising, and I got her in trouble too, sometimes. But I never got into the same trouble twice. You can learn things even from being naughty. Indeed I found that you learn, by being naughty, the things you have to practise to be good. You learn what not to do—and how not to.

Mother used to make the loveliest gingersnaps, and keep them in a tight tin box in the sideboard, and we were forbidden to touch them, of course. But when I got them out Peggy would eat some, naturally. One day Mother caught us, very crumby and sticky-fingered, and smelling of ginger and molasses.

"What have my little girls been doing?" Mother asked.

We protested that we'd been doing nothing. Then Mother led us to a mirror and pointed out our crumby, sticky little mouths and hands. Peggy, being six, was wise enough to not attempt concealment.

"We've been . . . eating . . . gingersnaps," she owned.

"That's a good little girl, to confess it," Mother said.

And then Peggy, encouraged, added, "And I wouldn't have

done it Mama, truly, but Ben took 'em out and gave me some."

"Oh, but that's naughty—to tell tales of little sister. Mama must punish you both."

We were promptly put to bed to meditate on our sins, and I meditated to some purpose. "Crumbs" was one subject of my study. "When you eat anything that you shouldn't, you should always be sure to wash your face and hands." "Confess" was another. I thought about this most earnestly.

"Mama," I asked, when she was kissing us goodnight, "what is 'confess'?"

And she took advantage of the occasion to explain the nature and virtue of confession at some length.

"Is it confession if I tell you I—Oh Mama!—I broke a kitty yesterday—stepped on it and broke it!" I cried, eager to partake of the new virtue. But Mother was suspicious, as we hadn't any kitty at the time, and explained to me the evil nature of lying, as well as the value of confession and repentance.

Then I made a plan.

A few days after, Mother being in the kitchen, I again helped myself to gingersnaps and even induced Peggy to partake, explaining to her that we could wash our faces and hands and nobody would ever know. This we did, and went unsuspected, but later on, I "confessed" with great freedom and fervor, but carefully said nothing at all about Peggy's part of the misdemeanor. Under questioning she was made to admit her share in the offense, and this time I had great credit—both for confessing and for not telling tales; indeed Peggy got all the punishment for once, for Mother said she was older than I and more to blame.

She was over a year older, but that didn't count for much even then, to my active mind. Mother put the gingersnaps on the top shelf of the closet, but I didn't care; I had learned a lot from those sweetmeats.

The most awful thing in my world at that time was the behavior of Father, especially to Mother. Of course I didn't know then what it was all about, but I could hear how he talked and scolded until Mother would break down and cry, and then he would be severe with us too.

One of the strongest impressions of all my very early childhood is that of being awoken out of my first sleep one night by one of these quarrels. I sat up, big-eyed and frightened, in my crib. It was like an awful dream. Father came home just drunk enough to be ugly—of course I didn't know that then—and he was saying fierce, loud things to Mother, and Mother was crying.

"Answer me that, woman!" he was shouting at her when I woke up. "Answer me that! Are you dumb—or foolish—or both!"

She was crying so she couldn't answer, and he grabbed her by the arm, and she cried out, and I was so scared I fell out of bed. I was too frightened to cry, and they were both frightened because I lay so still, and Mother ran and Father ran and they picked me up and felt my arms and collarbones, and put liniment on my forehead, and comforted me when I did cry at last, and I went to sleep holding a hand of each, and Father humming "The Land o' the Leal."

Afterward I thought and thought about it, marveling at the sudden stop to that quarrel. And next time I saw Father being disagreeable to Mother I created a diversion by tipping over a small worktable. But to my surprise Father spanked me and even Mother was cross, and I was sent to bed prematurely.

I could hear them still quarreling, while Mother picked up the spools and things. He told her she didn't know how to bring up children. I remember that because I resented it so, even then.

So I meditated on the success of falling out of bed that time, and the failure of tipping over the worktable.

"It isn't the noise," I said to myself. "It was being scared. They thought I was hurt—dead maybe! That's it!" and the next time they had a real quarrel I fell down stairs—just as bumpy as I could and crying awfully. That worked all right. They ran and picked me up and got the liniment; but Father was still cross. He went away and slammed the door pretty soon,

— 15 —

and I think Mother must have had her suspicions, for I didn't hear any more real quarrels for some years. If any seemed impending, Peggy and I were sent off in charge of Alison MacNab, and all doors were shut. Alison would tell us stories until bedtime, always about Scotland.

You see, my grandfather was Scotch; Andrew Angus Mac-Avelly was his name, and Father was named after him. Mother was a Quaker from Pennsylvania, Benigna Chesterton, and I was named after her. But Grandpa MacAvelly's wife was an Italian woman—this is the most important part of it—a splendid, big, handsome Italian woman, and a lineal descendant of the famous Machiavelli family.

That's where I come in. I'm a Machiavelli, and proud of it. The Scotch name I have to wear outside, like a sort of raincoat, but my real name I always feel is Machiavelli, Benigna Machiavelli. I mean never to marry and change it.

Grandpa had a theory, Father told me, that his family, the MacAvellys, were the progenitors of the Italian Machiavellis, and he'd quote a lot of medieval history to prove it; he was a very learned man. But Grandma never would agree to it. You couldn't shake Grandpa in an opinion, though; he was Scotcher than Scotch, and argumentative. You ought to have heard my father tell of the arguments they had and how obstinate Grandpa was! I used to think it took two to be as obstinate as all that, but I didn't say so to Father.

You see, Grandpa was one of those long-nosed, long-upperlipped, long-foreheaded Scotch, learned, conceited, pragmatical and pigheaded to the last degree. I've seen his picture, and I know, because I've heard Father talk so much about him, when Peggy and I were little and Father was sometimes sober and good-natured.

Father thought the world of Scotland. To hear him talk you'd think it was the finest country on earth, and Edinburgh the finest city. He'd tell about Princess Street and the Castle until I could fairly see the green gulf with the hidden railroad, the steep "Auld Toon" and Arthur's Seat and even Holy Rood.

He told us about Grandma, too, a tall, statuesque creature, dumbly rebellious, hating Scotland, always intriguing to get back to Italy—but Grandpa wouldn't go. Finally she ran away. He didn't say a word or stir a foot, didn't mention it, just sat down and went on without her as if she'd never been there. Also he grew so cruelly disagreeable, Father said, that he ran away, too, to America, and when the old man died he left nothing but an unsalable little rocky place, too sterile for anything but a sheep run, too small for a hunting box. Old Hughie MacNab, Alison's father, lived on it somehow, and sent over about five pounds a year. You should have heard Father boast of the income from his estate in Scotland!

All he really inherited was his mother's good looks and a taste for scheming, and his father's unlimited capacity for argument—and usquebaugh [whiskey]. He didn't drink so much as to be an offense in public, but he drank a little all the time and was a continual offense in private.

I was about ten when I found out what was the matter with him. Yes, I was ten the June before, and this was in the winter sometime, because the cars were heated. I remember how hot the seat was under me, and my feet seemed too big for my rubbers. The cars were full; it was a rainy night, and I was squeezed up against Mother, and a man was squeezed up against me. He was pretty red in the face and was disputing incessantly, first with one passenger and then another.

"Mama," I whispered, "is it polite to talk loud in the car?"

"Sh!" she said, looking frightened. "No, dear, it isn't. But keep still—don't notice him."

I couldn't help noticing, however, he made so much disturbance, and he smelled so, too. Presently he began to harangue a stern-looking woman with a short skirt and a man's soft hat, and she promptly replied, "Better be quiet, my man, else we shall think you're drunk."

He was still for a minute, looking rather redder, and

then said: "Why did you think I'm drunk, madam?"

"Because I can smell the whiskey on your breath," she answered, quite confidentially. "And because you talk too much. Just keep still and the others may not notice it."

He kept still, and so did I, but I was thinking hard. I knew the smell—I had often noticed it when I kissed Father—and I knew the color, and I knew the talk but I had never known what it came from before. Whiskey I had read about in Sunday School books, and drunkenness, and lovely little girls who had reformed their fathers, and a glorious ambition surged through me. I felt quite proud to have a Drunken Father like those heroes of fiction, and determined then and there to reform him. But on consulting the books I found that the literary variety of intoxicated parents either became violent and beat their families, in which case the angelic daughter took the blow and died like little Eva, or he lay breathing stertoriously on railroad tracks, and the angel daughter flagged the train with a flannel petticoat and again died gloriously—the agonized and repentant parent signing the pledge on the spot.

I could smell my father's breath most any evening, and I watched eagerly for a chance to save Mother from his violence. But there wasn't anything dramatic about Father's drinking; it didn't focus. All he did was talk and talk and talk, argue and dispute and wear Mother out.

Finally I thought it looked bad enough to give me a chance. Mother was quite broken down and ready to cry; Father was getting closer and closer and talking louder and louder. They didn't either of them know I was in the room. But I was sitting in the bay window, reading as long as it was light, and then thinking, and they didn't see me at all when the lights were lit. I was behind the curtain.

So I mustered all my courage, and rushed forward. It usually said in the stories : "She threw herself between them." I never quite mastered the mechanics of this throwing oneself, but I just ran between them and put my arms around Mother's neck, and said, "Talk to me, Father, not to Mother!" Well, he did. He talked to me for what seemed hours and hours.

I cried enough for twenty, but it didn't seem to help Mother a bit—she cried, too.

"You conceited little ass!" Father said. "You precocious little monster, with your brains all addled with preposterous story books! Why should I not talk to your mother, Miss Interference? Answer me that!"

It wasn't any use to answer, or to explain. Father went right on. I don't remember that he had ever really turned that caustic tongue of his and those interminable arguments on me before, and one thing I determined, as I stood scorching there, and that was that he never should again.

Mother told me afterward how wrong and foolish it was for me to criticize a parent, but she needn't have. I had learned my lesson.

It took me several months to win back Father's favor. He used to tease me cruelly about my "rescue work," but I took it all as medicine, and, though the course was severe, it was useful; I made it useful. You see, I had read about that Spartan boy with the fox gnawing his vitals, and envied him his grit even while I disbelieved the story. Also the Spartan spear story—training the boys to use extra big ones, so that the real spear, to the man's hand, should seem "as a feather." And the savages, too, with their awful ordeals—the things they used to do to the boys when they were admitted among the men.

The Ordeal theory always appealed to me very strongly, and, while I had no fox to gnaw my vitals, I used to practise with mosquitoes. I'd keep perfectly still and let them suck and sting and swell up with my blood, visibly. They were easier to kill afterward, too. Once I let a bee sting me, but that was worse; it hurt so I plastered mud on it pretty quick. And when Mother put our winter flannels on us too soon, which she always did, I used to play it was a hair shirt.

So when Father was horrid to me I would say to myself, "This is an Ordeal." And I'd stand it. I had to stand it, you see, anyway, but by taking it as an Ordeal it became glorious. And not only glorious, but useful. I was astonished to find, from those mosquitoes and things, that a pain isn't such an awful thing if you just take it as if you wanted it. And when

Father rebuked me, and was so sarcastic and tedious, even while it really hurt, and the tears ran down my cheeks, I would be thinking inside: "How foolish it is to keep talking after you've really made your point."

If you have an active mind, a real active mind that likes to work, there is profitable experience in most everything.

School was in some ways a better place to learn things than at home. I don't meant the study in the schoolbooks—a little of that goes a long way—but the things you can learn about people, and how to manage them. At first school seems very impressive, so big and busy, so many children, so many rules. But you get used to it.

I remember once, when I was about eight, sitting there with my lesson all learned, and thinking. It was a reading lesson, and I never did see the sense in those. Why, if you could read, you could read, and that was all there was to it. I always read the reader through as soon as I got it, and it wasn't half as nice as a real book, anyway.

The others were studying their lessons, however, and the big room was very still, all but the dull buzz children make when they are studying. I sat there and wondered why we had to maintain that oppressive silence. "Suppose we talked out loud," I thought. "What would happen? Suppose I did? I'm going to—just to see."

Then I cast about in my infant mind for the shortest word I knew, and all at once, across the dull murmur of the quiet schoolroom, rose a clear young voice saying, "It!"

The teacher was much astonished, for I was usually a model pupil. "Who said that word?" she demanded.

"I did," I said. She called me up to the desk and put her arm around me.

"Why did you do that?" she asked.

"I wanted to see what would happen," I answered.

And I found out. Nothing happened. She gave me a mild reprimand and told me not to do it again, which was needless;

I wasn't going to. I'd found out what I wanted to know.

It is easy to please a teacher, and you don't have to be very smart either. You only have to be "good," that is, keep the rules. If you want to do something extra, and have a real good record behind you, you can mostly do that, too. Then if you keep watch you can find out something the teacher especially likes—and perhaps you can get it for her or him.

Most of the scholars brought Teacher flowers, all kinds of flowers. I noticed that she always kept the roses most carefully, and if there were pinks she wore them. So I persuaded Father to put in some pinks for me next year, in my little bed down at the end of the garden, and I used to take one to Teacher every morning while they bloomed.

Teachers are easy—and there's only one of them. The children, they are harder.

But I kept my eyes open. I noticed who were the favorites, and why; who were the ones they didn't like, and why; and of those whys which of the good ones I could adopt and which of the bad ones avoid. As to studying, if you know your lessons pretty well, that pleases Teacher. If you know them too well, then the children don't like it. The girl they disliked most was at the very head. Teacher didn't like her, either—I could see that, for all she got the best marks. But if you know your lessons well enough to be able to help the others some, well enough to keep up but not well enough to get too far ahead, that pleases everybody. It's easier, too, and more amusing. I was quick enough at lessons, but I found time to sharpen pencils for ever so many others, and to do lots of things beside.

With the children just playing, I found that the thing they liked best of all was somebody who said, "Let's do this," and "Let's play that." So I used to think up things to do, and learn games on purpose—and make them up.

One year—I was about eleven then—we had a real nice teacher, but I think she was poor. She had a pretty little watch, only silver, but real pretty, and big Lucy Harrison knocked it off the desk one day—she was always clumsy. Then she turned around and stepped on it—backward—off the platform—with her heel—and broke it all to smash. Miss Arthur turned white. Her eyes filled with tears, but she comforted Lucy, who was bawling, said it was only an accident—didn't blame her a mite.

I made up my mind that Miss Arthur should have another watch—I didn't know how to do it, but I was bound I would—for Christmas. So I asked to see the pieces, and was ever so sorry about it, asked her if it couldn't be mended. She said no, but that she would get another some day. I noticed that the one she got was what the boys have—a "tin watch"—and she had to set it by the clock almost every day. The one that broke was marked "Longines."

I went to the best jeweler's store and asked how much a watch like that would be—I picked out one like it but prettier, and the man said ten dollars. That seemed impossible at first. But there were fifty children in our room, and two months to Christmas. I did it on my slate—fifty children into ten dollars—in long division, and it was twenty cents apiece. I didn't think they could bring twenty cents apiece even if they wanted to. But there were two months yet.

First I formed a Society, a Secret Society, to get Miss Arthur a Christmas present. I got Lucy elected President and myself Treasurer. Lucy was so sorry about the watch she contributed a quarter herself. We were all to bring five cents apiece to each meeting until we had money enough. The meetings were every Friday before school in the yard. But a month went by and I hadn't but seven dollars, and the other children seemed to have lost interest.

Then I got up a show, in our yard, a Dramatic Entertainment, which was to be five cents admission. Peggy and I used to perform "We Were Two Sisters of One Race." We loved it. "She was the fairest in the face"—that was Peggy. "They were together and she fell"—Peggy used to fall beautifully, just as flat, and not hurt herself, either. I used to wonder why he didn't hold her up, they being together. "Therefore revenge became me well"—I did the revenging. That was a great performance, really.

Peggy was the Earl, too, coming to my banquet, and the mother was just a bolster dressed up and a coif on—sort of bowed over, as was natural with a dead son in a sheet dragged in and laid at her feet like that.

And we did "The Outlandish Knight," too. I was the Knight, and Peggy, being bigger, could "Catch me round the middle so small and tumble me into the stream" with great effect.

I knew Father wouldn't like this, but it seemed to me a case of justifiable—well, I don't know what to call it. It wasn't disobedience. Neither Father nor Mother had ever forbidden my giving a dramatic entertainment. But it had to be planned very carefully. I wrote out quite a lot of cards announcing it, and gave them to the children in the different rooms that morning. Then I asked Dr. Branson and Mr. Cutter, and my Sunday School teacher. Their five cents were as good as anybody's. They came, too, and put in whole quarters. They said it was well worth it.

I took a day when father wouldn't be home until late. He had to go out of town somewhere. Peggy and I didn't need to rehearse much. Mother was persuadable. I asked her if I might have some children to come and play with us that afternoon, and she was willing. She knew we didn't often have a chance of that sort. She had to go downtown, she said, but we could play in the garden.

Of course, Alison was astonished to see so many, but I took her into my confidence to some extent, and she was much interested.

They came and they came and they came, and sat in rows on the grass. Peggy was scared, but I wasn't a bit. I had it all fixed up with Lucy Harrison, she being so big and the President. As soon as there was enough money she was to go down the street and get that watch—it was all picked out at the jeweler's—and to keep it until Christmas. Lucy could keep a secret, even if she was clumsy. The others of our Society didn't know yet what the present was going to be, so they couldn't tell.

Well, the performance was grand. And so many came that we had $12.75 in all. Before Mother got back Lucy had gone for the watch, and she got a pretty little hook pin for it, too, and religiously kept it until Christmas. Miss Arthur was so pleased when Lucy gave it to her. "From her loving pupils"— Minnie Arnold made a nice little speech. Minnie was the best orator we had. And Lucy presented the watch, because she had broken the other. I just sat in my seat and smiled.

Father was awfully angry with me. But it was too late. He couldn't do anything to Lucy Harrison, you see, and the thing was done. He punished me, of course; I had expected that—that was an Ordeal. But I think he could have hung me up by the thumbs without my being sorry. I felt so fine to think of Miss Arthur's really having that watch—a ten-dollar watch, and a nice pin—out of nothing at all. She praised Minnie and thanked Lucy, and she thanked "all her dear children," and I just grinned to myself for days, I was so pleased, and I felt proud, too, and longed for new worlds to conquer.

CHAPTER TWO

It was a world that I set my heart on next—a real world, a big globe for the schoolroom.

Mr. Cutter had a globe in his study so big I couldn't touch hands around it. The first time I saw it I was so pleased. It made the maps seem connected and sensible somehow. I could see how big Asiatic Russia was, and how little England was, and how Alaska leaned over to Japan and all sorts of things that never looked that way in the geography. Especially how things came together at the poles, like the knitting at the top of a mitten. And it would whirl around. It seemed to me we ought to have one in school.

I asked Teacher about it, and she said she'd love to have one, but they were not provided by the Board. I asked if the Board provided the geographies, and she said yes, they decided what we must have and the parents bought them. Did they provide the pictures on the walls? No, the "Art in Schools Society" did that. I used to wish that there were some children in that Society.

Now our minister thought well of me, and so did the Sunday School teachers. I used to go to Sunday School always, and was great friends with the teacher of our class. She liked me most, I think, on account of the paralyzed washerwoman. You see Jenny Gale next door told me their washerwoman was paralyzed and couldn't come any more, but she had a little grandson who brought the washing and took it. She was only half paralyzed, Jenny said, and could do about half as much washing as she could before, but she had to do it at home. I was tremendously interested, and persuaded Jenny to take me and go with the grandson, who was a solemn little boy, and see this mysterious half-disease. It made me think of that Prince with the black marble legs, she being black and all. Well, there was the poor old woman, able to hobble about and use one arm all right and the other a little (it was an up and down half, I found); and she had nothing to live on but her work, she and the grandson. They lived in a little garret sort of place, and it was four dollars a month. Now our Sunday School class was pretty big. There were always over ten there, and we used to bring nickels and dimes every Sunday, for Missions. I had asked about those Missions, and found it was mostly poor people, but the children didn't care particularly about them. They did not know them personally, you see.

I told our teacher, Miss Ayres, about this paralyzed washerwoman. I persuaded her to go and see her, and I said: "Oh please, couldn't we give *her* our money every week?" So then Miss Ayres suggested that perhaps our class could make a special mission of her rent. She was greatly pleased and interested. She took the whole class to see the old woman, and after that they used to bring dimes every Sunday and what there was over the rent we spent on Christmas presents for the grandson.

Anyway I was great friends with the minister, and when I asked him if it would disturb him if I came in sometimes and did my geography by his globe, he let me do it. So I got my nose in.

That idea came from the camel book. Peggy and I had a picture book about a Peasant in a Hut, and an Encroaching

Camel that asked to warm his nose, and then poked his head in, and gradually got inside and lay down by the fire and took up all the room, and the Peasant couldn't get him out. The trouble with that story, to my mind, was that camels live in countries that are warm—too warm. Whoever heard of a camel wanting to lie by a fire! And the Peasants in camel countries don't have huts, they have tents. However, lots of stories were queer. One had to take them as one found them. And I got the idea out of this one all right.

I used to be so quiet, just sitting there by the globe, never making any trouble, and he didn't notice that I came oftener and oftener. Then I asked if I might bring one of my schoolmates, promising to make no noise or disturbance. "She's very slow at geography," I told Mr. Cutter, "and the globe makes it so much clearer."

"Why don't they have one at the school?" he asked, laying down his pen and looking interested.

"I don't know," I said. "I wish they would. May I bring Carrie? We'll be very quiet. It's not every day, you know."

He let us. It was only in the afternoon. So the camel got his head in.

Well, Mr. Cutter, poor man, soon found a flourishing geography class trailing into his study Mondays, Wednesdays, and Fridays—a whole camel. I picked out children, though, who were in his church, and very polite and still, and I wasn't much surprised when it came Christmas to have Teacher announce that good Mr. Cutter had presented our room with this beautiful globe. It was a great comfort to the whole room, and other rooms used to borrow it, and by and by there were more of them. Perhaps it was a comfort to Mr. Cutter, too. In my own mind I used to call that globe my camel.

School things and church things, that is Sunday School ones, were not very difficult. Somehow where there are numbers of people together just for one purpose, sort of classified, it does not seem so hard to manage them.

I put that down in my diary when I was about twelve. I took more interest in my diary when I was young than I do now. Of course I know older people would laugh at that the way they do, and ask what I call myself now. And I know that chronologically (that's old enough, I hope) I'm what they call "only a girl." But if thinking makes people grown up, why I was older when I was fifteen than they are at fifty.

Why already, looking over these childish diaries and beginning to write out the earlier part of my life (so as to have "the decks cleared for action"—all the big crowding action that I can feel coming so fast), I feel not only old, but sort of immortal. As if life ran by, faster and faster, and I just stood watching, and sticking my finger in now and then. It is such fun!

Well, as I was saying, some things you can do easily. Others are harder. Some you can't seem to do at all. I found my hardest things at home. That is, there was one hard thing, big and troublesome. I couldn't seem to manage it at all—I mean Father.

Peggy was all right. She was pretty and good, and so obliging that she did not have to be managed. She was a great comfort to Mother at home, and I think Father liked her the best on account of her being so pretty. Or he would have if I hadn't taken extra pains.

I began to study Peggy very early, for she was always there. Father was away daytimes mostly, and even Mother was out sometimes, and downstairs in the evening, but Peggy was always with me, night and day. Naturally she was asleep nights, but so was I. So long as I was awake, there was Peggy. I was even in her room at school, for we were pretty nearly of an age, you see, and she was always willing to help me with my lessons.

So I gave my mind to the subject of Peggy from the first. Why was she prettier than I was? That I used to wonder when I wasn't five. But I admired her prettiness with all my heart, and loved her dearly. She was sweet-tempered and docile and popular, not like other pretty sisters I read about in story books, and we grew up very close together.

But as I got older—and I did get older far faster than she

did—my respect for her as older sister began to dwindle, and instead of looking up to her for her age and her good looks, I began to look down on her a little, because she wasn't as strong as I was intellectually. And then I got over that and began to see that for patience and sweetness and being a darling she was far superior to me. How one does change as one grows older!

But I was stronger really, so I secretly called myself "big sister" and learned to take care of Peggy in lots of ways. She loved, bless her dear heart, to "help little sister," as she had been told to from our babyhood, and she took great pains to have me keep up with her in school. She never noticed when I caught up with her, nor when helping me became the easiest way to learn her own lessons. As to getting ahead of her, I never did. That would have been a poor return for all her patience and kindness.

It's wonderful how much you learn by teaching people— that I soon found out. We kept together, year by year, and people praised her for helping me along far more than they did me for keeping up. That was lovely. I just danced inside, for I loved to have them praise Peggy, and above all things I wanted to be smart without being thought so.

When I was very little I took advantage of her sometimes, like that about the gingersnaps, but not afterward. As a matter of fact, when she did once in a while get into trouble, I could help her out and did, gladly. She was nicer than any other girl's sister I knew.

Then there was Mother—dear, blessed Mother. She was just all goodness. Such an unselfish sweet person I never saw, nor one so anxious to do what was right at any cost. Even Father admitted that, when he had to.

But Mother, for all her goodness, was just like the good people in the story books: she hadn't enough sense. It did seem, sometimes, as if she hadn't what Alison called "common wit," at least about Father. With us children she was wonderful, a real educator, but with him, it seemed as if her duty and unselfishness absolutely blinded her.

And I suppose, much as I love Mother, I have to admit,

if this is going to be what they used to call "a veracious chronicle," that even goodness—without sense—is sometimes wearying.

We young ones, sitting at the table, told severely by Father that we should be seen and not heard, kept quiet enough, and saw, as well as were seen. We saw a lot, even Peggy. "Little pitchers have long ears," Father used to tell us, and, "Children pick up words as pigeons peas, and utter them again as God shall please." I know that I picked up ever so many, and haven't uttered them yet.

Anyway we had to see and hear all dear Mother's patient, futile efforts to keep that father of ours good-natured. I suppose nobody really could have done it, but as early as eight or nine years old I used to think of things to say—and to *not* say—that I really do feel would have been wiser.

Of course Father was aggravating. But then he was a fixed fact. He had been a fixed fact to her ever since she married him. Surely what I, as a child, could learn in five or six years, at least two of which didn't count for much, she, being a grownup, ought to have learned sooner.

I used to sit there, "looking like a young owl," Father often said, listening to him and Mother, and thinking hard. I learned *very* young indeed that thinking was quite a different process from speaking. As a mere baby I would naturally say what I thought, but I soon found it was safer not to. If you say a thing, it is done, somehow, and nothing more happens. I mean even when you are not laughed at, or praised or punished, it's just said—and that's all. But if you think it, and bite hard, don't say a single word of it, it kind of pushes. The people in the stories, the sort of people I admired, used to think a lot and never say anything until "the time was ripe."

Why is it that people seem to imagine children cannot think? They can. I was only about eight when I discovered what a wonder-world was open to one's mind, nothing to do but walk in.

Father always insisted on our going to bed at the stroke of the clock, a very early stroke, too. If there was time after supper and if he was in a sufficiently good humor, he would read to us; he dearly loved to read aloud. That was about the pleasantest thing we have to remember about Father—reading aloud in the evening, that is, when the things were interesting. Scott was interesting. Scott's poems he read to us, and Scott's novels, and old Scotch ballads. They were among the very earliest things.

But you take a child with an active mind, or any mind at all, for that matter, stir it up with literature and then clap it into bed, why, that child does not always go to sleep. I know I didn't, nor even Peggy, at first. I'd lie there and make up stories and lovely things that might happen, as long as she would listen, and then, when she was really sound asleep, I'd go on and think them to myself. If I had my wishes! That was the usual beginning. Whether it was a fairy godmother or a magic ring—any sort of a starter—then the world was open. That old story of the husband and wife who had three wishes and wasted them all on a pudding. How I did despise that story. The poor, shortsighted idiots!

I used to begin by wishing that all my wishes might be wise and right and bring only happiness. Then I was safe, and could go ahead without feeling anxious about consequences.

At first this was so pleasant that I felt sure it must be wrong. That is one of the things children's minds are deeply impressed with, if they are brought up as we were—that nice things are pretty sure to be wrong.

Father was awfully strict and puritanical. When he read Burns to us (we didn't like Burns half so well as Scott, but Father praised him to the skies always), that about "the unco guid" always made me think of Father himself. At least it did when I was old enough. I can see now that all his conduct at home seemed perfectly right to him. Since I know more of life I can see that from most people's point of view he was an unusually good man, and from his own, quite perfect. He did all the Bible commandments right, the ten, that is. Nobody seems to pay much attention to the last two. And as to being tedious and stingy and domineering and argumentative and ill-tempered and dictatorial and satirical, why, there's nothing in the ten commandments about any of those things. It does say later on: "Fathers provoke not your children to wrath," but I guess that is only a very little commandment.

I've heard Mother ask him for money—when she had to, just *had* to—to buy thread to sew our clothes with. He'd argue about it, and want to see her accounts. Poor Mother. Just to ask for her account book was enough to make her cry almost. She had no head for figures, and he had. He had everything as clear as could be in his mind, and kept insisting on her keeping her expenses like that, and she really could not do it, though she tried. It wasn't, I can see now, that he *meant* to hurt her so much, but it was so hard on Mother!

I believe—this means now that I know so much more about life—I believe that people can be as brutal to each other's minds as they used to be in old times to their bodies. They can lash and burn and torture, they can cramp young brains as the Chinese do young feet, they can imprison and load with chains and starve and rack—all without its showing outside or anybody's blaming them.

And I've seen Mother wince when Father spoke to her just as if it were a whip. She'd set her teeth and turn white and hold her hands tight, other times; and pray, pray dreadfully, for strength to bear it, to be patient, to do her duty, to love, honor and obey. Of course she never dreamed I was under the bed.

To get away from all this and think things into shape—make everything all right in my mind—was a great relief, as you can well imagine. So I used to lie there nights and arrange it all in my mind—what I'd do if I had my wishes. I would be perfectly beautiful, of course, and so wise and good! Mother should grow well and happy and have all the lovely soft clothes she wanted—gray and lavender and pale rose and pearl, the colors she liked best. And she should have money, all the money she wanted, and we would refurnish the house from top to bottom—I had heard her wish for new furniture.

The furniture, and Mother's clothes, and Peggy's and mine, too, used to last me interminably. I always got to sleep before the last rooms were done, or the wardrobe.

Then there was the splendid margin of Giving Away. We had a sort of Fortunatus purse, of course, and all the poor people we knew became quite comfortable at once.

And when I was particularly angry about something, there were hours of fearful pleasure spent in doing things to my enemies. I always enjoyed that part of the fairy stories, when the wicked sister was put in a barrel set with knives and rolled down hill. Children certainly are cruel.

For Father I never was quite sure what to do. Mostly I changed him, changed him so that he was hardly recognizable, but so that we could love him. I always did want to love Father, but couldn't. Peggy did, though, I really believe.

But all that was only thinking. Daytimes I had to manage, if I could.

As for Alison McNab, nobody could have managed her, not the great Machiavelli himself, I am sure. She had nursed Father when he was little, and spanked him, and I am convinced she came to this country to look after him. She loved Mother dearly—she had to. But I know if she had not had caring for Father built into her constitution that way, she never would have put up with him.

Come to think of it, he never was as outrageous to her as he was to Mother. Alison had a sharp tongue and a cool head. I loved to hear her "answer back," always polite enough, and "knowing her place," but holding her own perfectly. And the Scotch dishes she cooked for him made her safe to keep the place, no matter what she said. Scones and shortcakes and brose and haggis and lots of queer things. Mother never caught the knack of it.

Once or twice I tried my hand on Alison, but she would fix those very small, very keen eyes of hers on me, and seem to see through my little devices.

"You're ower wise for one o' your years," she would say dryly. "I misdoubt you're ower wise altogether."

But then Alison always did what she ought to; I didn't have to manage her.

So at home, though Peggy and Mother were easy—real

easy—and Alison hard, the only practical difficulty was Father. He was the Master and Owner and Governor. He "commanded and forbade and released prisoners and remitted the customs taxes" like the sultans in the stories, only mostly he imprisoned and put the taxes on.

Father had severe ideas of discipline and how children should be "trained." People act as if children were performing dogs or horses, or something that has to be "broken." Mother felt very differently. She had studied to be a kindergarten teacher before Father married her; she really cared about children and making them happy. But Father scorned "all these morbid modern follies of child-culture" and used to take pleasure in ridiculing and abusing Mother's ideas. He wouldn't let us go to a kindergarten, but he couldn't help mother's teaching us in the nursery in that wise way, so we really had some advantage of it.

I think Mother was too easy with us, partly to offset his severity, but we soon learned how to change our behavior as soon as Father's key turned in the lock. I noticed that if we did anything he disapproved of he always blamed Mother for it, showing at great length how our misconduct was due to her false ideas.

Now I would often have done as I liked and taken my punishment—a punishment is only a price, it doesn't kill you. But I hated to hurt her.

I read in one of my story books of a strange, precocious boy who read Emerson. So I read Emerson too, or tried to, as early as twelve or thirteen. Some of it I could understand, and it was good sense.

"'If you want anything, pay for it and take it,' says God." That struck me as reasonable.

I used to figure up what a thing would cost, and whether I could afford it or not, and if it hadn't been for Mother, I think I could have indulged in far more liberties. But I couldn't afford to have Mother hurt any more than she had to be.

As I grew up I noticed more and more how horrid Father was to Mother, and one of the problems I set myself to work out was how to . . . well how to mitigate him. I couldn't stop him, I couldn't take Mother away, or Peggy. But there are always ways. I'd say to myself: "Now suppose he were a Giant or an Ogre—and had us—what could I do to outwit him?" Or, "Suppose he were an Enemy, and had us in prison, or enslaved. What could I do for Mother and Peggy?" Opposition was out of the question, or Conquest, or Escape. Wives and children can't escape, it appears. I tried to think that out, but gave it up.

Once I went to Mr. Cutter about it. In George MacDonald's books the minister does such wonderful things with families, always. Mr. Cutter was very kind, but he didn't seem to appreciate the point of view at all.

"My dear little girl," he said to me, "a child has no right to criticize her parents. You read too many story books with that active brain of yours. Your business is to study your lessons and obey your parents. You are getting morbid, my dear."

You see, he didn't know. When he called, Father was polite enough; and I dare say he was to strangers, generally; and as to his treatment of us, well I guess I didn't make it clear. People didn't know he drank either, and they thought he was a "good family man" because he stayed at home evenings. And as he didn't beat us until we screamed, nobody knew what we suffered. Peggy minded it least. She had a sunny temperament and was unobserving. At school she was very successful and well liked, and she didn't do things Father disliked at home. I didn't either, but then I wanted to, and felt the restrictions.

I don't think Peggy ever realized how much Mother suffered either, or half appreciated the bitter satire and veiled condemnation with which he talked to her, right before us. And I guess she slept sounder than I did and didn't hear him keeping Mother awake nights with his long-drawn-out faultfinding. I heard him. I used to lie and clench my hands and shut my teeth tight, and get madder and madder. I could see so easily how Mother could have made it better for herself, in several ways.

But dear Mother had no vestige of diplomacy. She would provoke him when it wasn't necessary, interrupt him when he was nearly through and have to hear it all over again; submit where she needn't have, and resist when it was no use. Poor little Mother.

One thing Mother loved dearly was flowers. We had a big yard and a vegetable garden, and every year she would beg him to let her have tulip beds, and set out roses and so on, and he would not have it. She liked to have flowers all around in the house and on the table and on herself, and Father got the idea that this was unhygienic. Also I think it was partly contrariness, just because Mother urged him at inopportune moments, and once he had taken a stand he wouldn't ever give up.

I observed this; it flashed across me all at once when I was nearly twelve, that they had this discussion every spring.

I had kept a diary since I was eight. One of the things I most often put down was: "Father scolded Mother," or "Father quarreled with Mother," and usually, "about flowers" or "about visitors" or "about us children" or "about money"— whatever it was about. So now I looked over these diaries and sure enough, this was an annual quarrel about flowers.

It seemed such a simple, nice thing, too, for Mother to have a garden to suit her. She had very few things as she liked them. It would be good for her health, I knew. And I began to wonder if this one thing couldn't be managed; if I could get around Father in this it might help in bigger things. So I studied earnestly about it.

There was his Scotchness—that ought to be a help. And his funny mixture of parsimony and then suddenly spending all the money there was in some plan of his, when we needed coal or the market bill was crowding. If only *he* could be got to want the garden—and Mother would keep still and let me work it!

I had read in several story books of Scotch gardeners, always Scotch gardeners, and it used to astonish me as much as their making marmalade in that country. Why orange marmalade should be made in a land where there are neither oranges nor sugar was always a mystery to me. Indeed it is yet. I'd as soon look for guava jelly from Siberia, or canned peaches from Greenland. However, there did seem to be something in this Scotch gardening idea. I began to besiege the nice man at the public library for books on gardens and gardening, especially Scotch; and such as were interesting I'd take home and read. I'd read extracts to Mother or Peggy.

When Father was good-natured, I'd ask him how to pronounce this or that queer Scotch name, and if he'd ever been to such a place, and if it was true that Lord Hiltover had the finest flowers in all Britain, and if he knew the Edinburgh man who got the prize for roses in three successive seasons. Then he'd look at the pictures and get interested, and talk about Scotland, as he was always ready to do, and to encourage us in studying anything Scotch—I knew that. Then I found a book on "Scientific Gardening for Profit" and began to try to figure out the sums in it. They didn't come out right—I wasn't very careful—and then I'd say, "Oh, Father, this Mr. McVeigh says he can raise so many roses off so many feet of ground—just working at it evenings—and I've done it and it doesn't come out half so many." Then he'd scold me, say I had no head for figures; take up the quarrel as earnestly as if he were Mr. McVeigh himself.

"How much land is that?" I'd ask. "Is it twice as much as our yard?"

No, he said, it was not. We had more, in fact.

"Well anyhow," I persisted, "I don't believe he could do it in that much time; he must have hired someone to do the real work. Or perhaps he was an exceptional man— a real genius. Nobody could really raise such flowers on that much land now. See," I showed him, "he says here that he began in the autumn to prepare for his rose garden and by the next summer he counted so many hundred blossoms on the first planting. Do you think it could be done, Mother?"

Then Mother took a hand just as I hoped she would, disputing the statements of Mr. McVeigh. She said she had tried it in Pennsylvania and it couldn't be done—and that the climate was better there than it was here, and far better than in Scotland she was sure.

Then Father rose to the occasion and argued—for hours. He said the Scotch were the greatest gardeners the world had ever known, and cited their triumphs by the score. He said women had no capacity for handling tools or raising flowers, let alone vegetables, and that they had not brains enough to see the truth in plain figures given by an intelligent and experienced man.

"Here is this conceited, ignorant young Miss" (he meant me of course, and I looked as miserable as I could), "disputing this clear and rational statement. I shall take pleasure in showing you that this thing can be done, madam, exactly as Mr. McVeigh says."

You see, Father was nothing if not scientific; he was always planning things—things that never succeeded, to be sure. But he kept on planning. So now *he* launched out in books on gardening, bought big ones that we couldn't afford, and cuttings and slips and seeds, and bulbs; set up hot beds; and was forever fussing around in the garden in the long summer evenings. By next spring we did have quite a garden, and in two or three years it was lovely. He didn't work at it much after the first year, and he wouldn't let Mother have flowers in the house, but the garden was there all the same. And Mother got lots of comfort out of it.

CHAPTER THREE

They say that if horses only realized their strength we could not manage them as we do. That is true enough; anybody can see it. What we never learn—at the time, I mean—is that if children realized their strength we could not manage them as we do, either.

Perhaps it is just as well, for most children seem to have so little sense. Sometimes I feel as if I would like to start a Revolution among children, but then when I see how foolish they are, it is discouraging.

For instance, every child has to suffer from the clothes put on him or her. The more loving and careful parents are, the more underflannels and overcoats and rubbers and things they pile onto the children. Such thick cloth, too!

Why, you'll see poor, fat, toddling things in coats of stiff, heavy stuff, thicker than their fingers; so still and heavy that the poor child cannot bend her or his arms. How would a grown person like to wear a coat stiffer and thicker than a door-mat, so that they stood there in a barrel, a hot woolly barrel, with arms that wouldn't shut? The parents pile on what they see fit, and the children have to put up with it.

I didn't.

If they put on more clothes than I wanted, I practised passive resistance—simply sat down and stayed there.

"Please take it off!" I said. "*Please* take it off. *Please* take it *off!*" And I wouldn't move until they did. They could carry me, but that was tiresome. You can punish a child, of course, but if the child is willing—quite polite, but determined—you can't punish them forever.

"You were the most stubborn baby!" Mother used to say. "I'm so glad you are more reasonable now, Benigna."

I am. She does not dream—dear Mother!—how very reasonable I am.

But most children certainly are not.

My efforts were quite a good deal interfered with by having to conceal my real character. That makes life more interesting, but more complicated, too. When I was really a child I didn't know enough for this, and got a reputation for being "too clever," "sly," Alison called it. I soon found that had its disadvantages.

Then, for years, I tried my best not to seem clever. It wasn't easy. If I just kept still they said I was "deep," and to talk, that is to talk like other children and not say what I wanted to, was quite hard. But that was interesting too.

At first, just to keep from being punished and disliked, I did it. Then as I grew older and began to see what I might do with my life, why then it was absolutely necessary.

You see, if people think you are "a schemer," as they call it, they are suspicious, and it makes it harder. My ambition is to be, to seem to be, that is, just like other people, and to do things—wonderful things—without ever being suspected of it. That's fun!

I had to realize very young that I was queer. That is, that I was different from other people. At first I just felt smart and proud; then when people talked about me, I learned how they felt about it. Isn't it astonishing the way people talk about children right before them? As if they were deaf—or idiots!

A child of three would have more sense than that—to say things right out before people, which she or he didn't want them to hear.

I suppose it was because I so much wanted people to like me that I tried so hard to please them, at first. But now that I am so much older I can reason it all out, and see that if I am to accomplish what I mean to, I have to have friends—any number of friends.

One can learn as much as that out of fables and fairy tales; Androcles and the Lion, The Lion and the Mouse, that one about the Prince, The Ant and the Fish—lots of them.

Then, as soon as I found out what a long, serious business it was going to be, I began to keep two diaries. There was the little one I started when I was a child of eight. Anybody could read that. It was in my little desk. I'm keeping it up, too, and it's about ten years now. But for the last six I've kept another that nobody ever saw. It was lots of fun hiding it.

The little one has facts in it. It is really very handy sometimes as a family record book, when they dispute about the day they started the furnace last year, or the date of the big snowstorm.

I used always to sit down after supper and write in it. Father would make caustic remarks, and Mother defend me, and dear Peggy come and kiss me and say she thought keeping a diary was real nice, she wished she could remember to do it.

Then in the precious minutes when I was alone, or when I was supposed to be writing something else in school I would put down what I really thought and felt, and hide it—like a spy with plans of the Enemy's Fortifications. If you have enormous interesting plans to carry out and are leading not only a double but almost a triple life, you *have* to have a way to free your mind.

Then I began this, a sort of story of my life, and when it is up to now I mean to destroy my second diary altogether.

The reason I want to write it—this, I mean—is partly self-consciousness, I suppose. I'm quite old enough to see that. But what of it? If you *are* big, you *have* to know it—there's no use pretending not to, to yourself, of all people.

There have been infant prodigies before now, in music, or arithmetic, or things like that. I was an infant prodigy in common sense, that's all; just plain intelligence, with, of course, that splendid Machiavellian streak thrown in.

I have a big, clear, definite Purpose now, a great, long one, stretching through life.

I mean to help people—all sorts of people, in all sorts of ways—*without their knowing it!* This is not philanthropy—not at all. Anybody can get rich, and give money to poor people. I don't mean that. There are plenty of rich people who need help—the kind I mean. Children with horrid parents, parents with horrid children, wives with horrid husbands, husbands with horrid wives, all kinds of workers who ought to have different work—who need encouragement and to be set in the right surroundings; good people to be nice to, and bad people to get even with. I do particularly love to get even with people, like a Corsican.

There was Mrs. Judson with her hens. That was a chance. It was ever so long ago—I must look in my little diary. Yes, here it is, innocent enough: "Shooed out Mrs. Judson's hens." That was all I put down.

I was eleven then. Those hens were a nuisance to us all the time. That was before I achieved the flower garden, but we had vegetables, and we children had a few flowers.

Those hens seemed to prefer our yard to theirs, and Mrs. Judson would not shut them up. She let them run in her big trodden yard, and when they wanted delicacies, they flew over the fence. We complained and protested, but she only got angry. We urged her to make her fence higher, but she wouldn't. I heard all the talk, of course.

Now, children, as I said before, can do a lot if they only realize their strength.

We had a sort of shed down at the end of the garden. Father used it as a tool house. It had a sliding door.

There were some boys in our room at school who liked me pretty well, because I'd read the Mayne Reid books and took an interest in them. I asked two, the Bentley twins, if they were afraid of hens. That made them laugh.

Then I told them to come to our shed Saturday afternoon at about three o'clock—not to tell anybody, but to be there, getting over the fence from behind.

Saturday afternoon Mrs. Judson always went downtown and so did Alison McNab. Mother would be lying down in the front room and Peggy, bless her, I could send on an errand of any length.

Jim and Teddy Bentley were very much excited over the plan, and came silently over the back fence at the right time.

I had fixed a string to the shed door and baited the place with corn (Five cents will buy a lot of corn). One of the boys stayed in the shed, scattering just enough corn to keep them interested; and the other one played tag with me, sort of naturally, but so as to keep the hens down at the lower end of the garden. Gradually, we got them all in the shed, crowding and gobbling, and shut the door.

"Now come on," I said, "and we'll take turns holding and cutting. We mustn't let them squawk."

Then one of us would grab a hen by the neck and legs. Not choking them, just so they couldn't squawk much; and one would hold out the wings, and the other cut. Only feathers, of course. It didn't hurt them any. As soon as one was done, it would go back to the corn—we kept sprinkling a little more now and then.

We worked fast, and it was very hot and feathery, but most exciting. When they were all clipped (and it took a good while to be sure—hens do look so alike), we took one at a time, holding it carefully and comfortably so it wouldn't squawk, and dropped it over Mrs. Judson's fence.

There were twenty hens and a big rooster, but it seemed like hundreds.

And then we weren't through.

"We've got to conceal the evidence of our crime!" I said. That was quite a piece of work. All those feathers to pick up— such a lot of them—and to bury. They were stiff feathers, you see, not the flying, fuzzy kind. We piled them on a big piece of paper, rolled them up hard, tied it up tight, and buried it deep, in the garden.

Peggy came back before that was done, but she didn't know what we were gardening so busily for. Alison saw us down there, but she was used to our games and did not suspect anything. The hens were all nosing around as usual on their own side of the fence, and some of them, poor things, were trying to get over again and couldn't.

Mrs. Judson noticed it in time, and I guess she had an idea who did it, but that didn't help the hens any. However, though I was proud enough then, and so were the boys, I soon felt ashamed of this performance.

In the first place, I had forgotten that feathers would grow again. In the second, I had quite overlooked the possible advantages of Mrs. Judson's hens. I didn't realize this until the next year. The fence had lost a few pickets (I think she pulled them off) and they came in worse than ever.

I didn't think of this advantage myself. I saw a verse in a newspaper:

> When your neighbor's hens
> Come across the way,
> Don't let angry passions rise—
> Fix a place for them to lay.

That was better, a lot better. I studied the best henhouses that any of our friends had, and asked intelligent questions. People seem always glad to tell a child things if the child is polite; they seem to feel complimented somehow.

The Bentley twins had a toolchest, and lots of old pieces of wood they had accumulated in their yard, and between us we made the best henhouse of the neighborhood out of our old shed.

Of course Father had to be persuaded to let us do it, and to let me keep the few Leghorns I could afford to buy out of my pocket money. He was horrid about it, but finally agreed. "My decoys," I called them. Alison let me have a good deal of stuff from the kitchen to help out in feeding, and Mother bought the eggs from me, at a little less than market price. She was astonished at the steady way my hens laid—an egg a day for each one, right along.

I was out early and late to get those eggs; and the extra ones—sometimes there were six or more that should have been Mrs. Judson's—the twins would go and sell to people. Nice people like to encourage children in earning money that way, and the eggs were new-laid.

It was this hen business which started me on my great plan of learning things. I was twelve—and I'm eighteen now. Six years. How much one can learn in six years.

That toolchest of the twins was a revelation to me. It was such fun, such gorgeous fun, to make things. At school they taught the boys to work in wood and metal and so on, but we girls could only cook and sew. At first this made me angry—not that I showed it—but later I saw the advantages. In the first place, you can get *some* brain exercise out of cooking and sewing. In the second place, the more things you can do the stronger you are; and in the third place, boys like to be cooked and sewed for. Mostly they despise girls, but I found that if a girl has sense, and isn't a silly coward, and can throw straight, they like them better. It is surprising how much boys think about throwing stones as a virtue. They say "girls can't throw stones," and grown people talk about their collarbones being different.

As for me, when we went to the seashore, I used to play "duck on a rock" with the other children, with relays of other children, until I got to be a regular sharpshooter. You'd think they wouldn't play with me if I were the best shot all the time, wouldn't you? Yes, but you can shoot at more things than the "duck." I only knocked that off about as often as they did, or a little less so; but I hit the pebble I aimed for, oftener and oftener.

You can learn to do anything, I found, just anything, if you give your mind to it, work steadily, and never get excited or discouraged.

When I was older I saw a thing that a man named Hunt said—William Hunt, an artist. "If you want to paint, *paint.*"

— 45 —

That's all. Just do it, do it anyhow, and by and by, you can!

Well, I meant to be able to do as many things as I possibly could, and as soon as I got well started on that, life became tremendously interesting. Now let me count back. There was the cooking and sewing. I didn't like them particularly, but they would help.

All they taught us in school I learned, and then began at home. Alison was hard to persuade, but I made a special study of her ways, noticed when she was extra tired or had a toothache, and began to do little bits of her work for her. How on earth people can be so stupid as to neglect this line of advantage I cannot see—not only foolish children, but foolish everybody. Here is a world full of people, and only one you. What you do to them is a small matter; what they do to you is a large matter—anybody can see that. And unless you are a towering genius or something like that, you *need* people, always, to help you.

Families come first, naturally, and, barring Father, I was doing pretty well with mine.

Not to be "too clever" with Alison. Not to be "too deep." To be quiet, mostly; and when I talked, to talk like other children—as far as I could. Story books were safest; one can repeat other people's stories without committing oneself to anything.

Little by little, I managed so that Alison liked me as well as she liked Peggy. I heard her admit to Mother one day: "Benny's none so bad. She's quite a help i' the hoose."

So I learned a lot, not just cooking, but all you do in a kitchen, and in general.

I asked to keep our room in order, Peggy's and mine, and used to practice on that in the way of dusting and putting things away. Dear Peggy was a scatterer, but the more she scattered, the more I put up. I wasn't angry with her, for you see I didn't care at all about the things, only about learning how.

To be quick, quiet, dexterous, neat—all the nice adjectives I read in books about maids and housewives. "Who knows when I may need it?" I said to myself. And sure enough . . . but that's a long way ahead.

Anyway I learned all that was in reach about housework, and managing, too; buying things and so on; and got leave now and then to make things like gingerbread or cookies or fudge. Of course, those things they'd let me give my friends, and when I came over into the twins' yard with a lot of hot, nice-smelling cookies, they let me use their tools some.

They let me play ball with them, too, in the yard, said I was "a good catch—for a girl." They never would admit that I could throw as well as they could, but I did all the same. What they admitted didn't matter, it was doing it.

Then in my second diary I began to make lists of all I could learn. As to school studies, they didn't interest me as much as real things, but I could see that some arithmetic was necessary—enough to keep accounts; I got that pretty thoroughly by helping Mother keep hers. Poor, dear Mother. She was glad enough to be helped.

Languages were of some use too, even the dead ones; at least Latin, if you want French and Italian and those.

When it came to the real live sciences—things that are so . . . that work, that you can see work—why those were just a pleasure.

Games are good, too, big games, like chess and whist. The one thing that I feel I have to thank Father for is that he played checkers and chess so well, and was willing to play with me.

I nearly spoiled it when I began to beat him. Mad! You never saw anybody so mad. He just couldn't stand it. Then he said he wouldn't play at all, and I was horrified and remembered my "duck on a rock" just in time.

"Just one more, Father!" I begged him. "For revenge, you know."

Well, he beat that one. And he beat most of the time after that, keeping one ahead always, but with me always near enough to make him a little anxious. Meanwhile I gained and gained. I could see my checkmates further and further ahead, and just at the proper moment I would make a misplay. I'd give him a pawn and learn to play just as well; a bishop, and work harder; a knight, and still keep up; a queen, and then get his. I played games within games, all splendid practice, and yet Father beat the most, and was satisfied.

He bragged of me, too, and sometimes had me play a game with friends of his; he liked me to beat them. So we got on very well, with proper care on my part.

And I began to see for myself, in my own practice, that it isn't the winning that matters, it's the game; it's learning how to play.

The best game of all was the big one—living. As I grew I began to see more and more of it: what fun it was, how wide and endless, and what poor players most people were. They had no plans at all, apparently, and no idea of rules beyond "second hand low, third hand high, fourth hand take it if you can."

Making people like you is a game. Learning to like people is a game. They work together too. You see at first I was really very much taken up with what went on in my own mind, and was inclined to be very critical about other people's foolishness. But I soon got the idea of pleasing people, as I've already put down, and later I saw the necessity of the other. "Why, they *are* people—that's all. This *is* the way they act. If I wait for a lot of wise, careful people to love I shall be very lonesome."

Then I'd write it down large—just for myself:
"What do I want to do in life?
"I want to be big—Big—BIG!
"I want to know everything—as far as I can.
"I want to be strong, skillful, an armory of concealed weapons. I want to be far more able than anybody knows.
"And then what? What am I to do with it?
"Play with people. Do things with them, and for them.
"And never be known!"
Then I'd tear that paper fine, or burn it.

I've forgotten to put down about the things I've learned already.

All those housekeeping things didn't count; they came in at odd minutes.

Sewing was better in a way: the science of it at school, the practice of it at home. I helped Mother with the mending. I made dresses for dolls for the Sunday School Christmas trees. I made dresses for poor children for the Sunday School sewing circle. I made aprons and petticoats and nighties and things. Then I got some cheap, pretty cotton stuff and made a housedress for Mother—a real pretty little one. She was so pleased. Just here and there, to keep my hand in, I made things, experimenting a good deal. Now I can do any kind of plain sewing, mend and darn well, and really cut out and make dresses. I don't propose to *do* it, as a business, but it's one step. While I was at it I got leave to take some regular lessons with Mrs. Folsom, a dressmaker who went to our church. That was to learn about workrooms, how they did it professionally. And I learned—a lot. The way they waste cloth, the way they take more orders than they can fill and keep putting people off, not having things done when they said they would. I made notes on Dressmakers in my secret diary.

Meanwhile I learned shorthand, just for fun. You never know when you may need a thing. There was a girl in school whose sister did it and she got her sister to lend me the books and help a little now and then. Peggy helped me in dictation, and I'd work at it while Father read aloud, or in church. I got used to Mr. Cutter's delivery, and when his secretary was sick I asked if I mightn't help him a little while, and got used to really doing it.

Then there was typing, of course. Father had a typewriter, but refused to let me touch it. He certainly was not a helpful parent, unless by calling out ingenuity.

It was perfectly absurd that I should have to fuss and scheme and go out of the house to learn, when it stood there all day, idle. So I made up my mind that I had a perfect right to use it, and began. First I carefully watched Father do it. Then I studied the book of directions very closely. My very first lesson, to myself, I managed one day when I was really alone in the house. That was a godsend. I had bought some cheap paper to practice on, and I put in a whole evening, in half-hour spells, with rest between.

Then I sat boldly down to it when only Alison was about. She didn't realize that it was forbidden, but suspected it. I didn't think she'd tell, and she didn't.

Peggy didn't, of course. But Mother was different. It frightened her to see me deliberately disobeying Father. She didn't want to tell him, of course, but she said it was a sin—disobedience. I quoted the text where it says: "Children obey your parents—in the Lord."

"Doesn't that mean there are times when you don't have to?" I asked. "I'm not doing the least harm, Mother. You can see how softly I work, and I've made such progress already. See? Now, don't you tell me not to, Mother dear, because it's not your machine and I don't believe Father'll really mind when he sees how nicely I can do it."

He caught me at it at last. He came home early one day, and, of course, he made an awful fuss. But I was quiet and gentle and polite—just stood there and let him tear up my sheet of paper and scold. I didn't say a thing, not a thing, except those little mild stave-off remarks you *have* to make. You see when a parent is angry, he scolds—or she, if it is some other girl's parent. And scolding is silly, always silly. I noticed that almost in infancy.

"What do you mean by doing so and so?" they shout—as if the child had deep-laid intentions. (As a matter of fact, I had, very often, but most children don't.)

"How many times must I tell you not to do that?" they demand furiously. I always felt like making an estimate, saying, "Eight," at a venture, or, "Fifteen." But if you try to reply to a plain question they call it "impertinence." Then they call names, complain of the trouble you make. Sometimes I've really heard them say, "I'm sure I don't know what to do with you," in a fierce voice, using their own failure as a club. Of course the child might say politely, "I'm sorry for that," or "Too bad," but they'd only catch it worse. But you have to say "Yes," and "No," and "I'm sorry," or "I won't do it again." If you say absolutely nothing it makes them more and more enraged. "Do you hear me?" they demand, knowing that you can't help it. "What have you to say for yourself?" or "Answer me this minute!" they yell.

Being scolded is like surf bathing—you have to know when to duck and when to jump. I was very skillful, because Father scolded so much.

Well, I wriggled through this scolding safely. When he got to a certain point I put my handkerchief to my eyes and ran out of the room. You mustn't do that too soon or you get called back and have to take it worse, but after a while you can—when you see that they can't think of much more to say.

Father stamped around quite a good deal that time, but he had to leave the house every day, and the machine only had a cloth cover. Before he caught me again I had really learned to do it. I looked up with a pleasant smile, and showed him my page with modest pride.

"See, Father," I said gaily, "I can do a page in twelve minutes now."

"I have forbidden you to touch that machine," he said. "You are a disobedient child—you. . ."

I was about sixteen then, and I smiled up in his face and said: "Please forgive me, Father. I know I was disobedient. I am very sorry to displease you." That was true, I wouldn't say I was sorry for disobeying—I wasn't. "But I have really learned to do it nicely. It can't hurt the machine, can it? And some day I may really need to know typewriting—girls do, you know. . . ."

He scolded quite a good deal, but I have noticed this: if you have really *done* a thing, if it is accomplished, then even a scolding person can't think of so much to say. Besides what they say does not matter—the thing is done.

CHAPTER FOUR

As I look back now at the things I did when I was twelve, they seem foolish enough. One does not know much at twelve, even a girl. And boys! How they do behave!

"Boys will be boys," people say in a fatalistic sort of manner, as if nothing on earth could prevent their acting that way. I wish I'd had a brother. He'd have been a boy, of course, but I'm pretty sure he'd have been a modified boy.

I knew plenty of boys quite intimately while I was a child, and made the most of my opportunities. When they got older and used to flock together more and refuse to play with girls, while at the same time they'd stand on corners watching them and talking about them, I lost my grip, to a certain extent.

The girls who were most popular with boys at that age were the dressy ones, pretty, and what I called foolish. But the boys liked them , that was plain. For some time I considered that line of action, whether it was worthwhile. Books are full of it, of course. Even as a child I could see that.

There was Becky Sharp—intelligent enough, but doing

things by such small methods! They all did. Even Jael and Judith seemed crude to me. There was that story in the Apocrypha—where the King set that riddle as to what was the strongest thing, and one said, "the sword," and one "wine," and one "the King," but the prize answer was "women." They could manage the King!

I examined this theory carefully. Wanting to be strong, as I did, to accomplish all sorts of things, I said to myself: "See here, if this is the best way really, I'll try it."

So I studied the matter. First I looked at the most successful ones as I knew them in real life. They were awfully foolish girls, as a rule. Some of them didn't seem to know what they were doing at all. You might as well praise honey for drawing flies. It didn't seem worthwhile to me.

Then I looked at the smart ones, those you read about in history, or in fiction, that had this wonderful power. Mary, Queen of Scots, had it, and much good it did her, poor thing. Helen of Troy had it. Cleopatra had it. No end of prominent women had it, but what did they do with it, and how did they come out in the end?

What I can't understand is how people can read history, or fiction, for that matter, and not learn anything. This attraction of theirs really is like honey—they only succeed in being eaten, after all. For another thing, all their wonderful power is so short-lived. It is only young ones who have it, apparently, and surely anyone knows youth doesn't last forever.

I was planning for life, a long life, with lots of fun. Why, it's no secret. Life *is* a long thing—if you don't die young— and *that* I never was afraid of.

Any child knows he or she is going to grow up—if they know anything. Any girl knows she's going to be a woman. Any woman knows she's going to be an old woman, if she doesn't die sooner.

But do we *do* anything about it? Not we. We all act as if time stopped by about day after tomorrow. Well, I am planning to live a long time, ninety or a hundred years, maybe, and I want to have fun *all* the time—not just between fifteen and thirty, or even forty.

So I concluded I'd rather miss that one kind of power and try for others that would keep.

When I was about fourteen I heard a woman doctor lecture on hygiene at our school. It didn't seem to have much effect on most girls, but I was tremendously impressed.

That was the beginning of my training, physical training, I mean. I set up a Goal in my secret diary. "I mean to be Strong," I put down. "As strong as I possibly can. And well, of course."

This is no mystery either. As to being well, that's easy. Air is the first thing—all the fresh air you can get. Peggy didn't like it, so I finally succeeded in getting a room to myself, namely the attic. There were windows at each end, and a skylight. It was big, with lots and lots of room, and high in the middle.

It was hot in summer, but heat isn't unhealthy if you have air, and it was cold in winter, but cold isn't unhealthy either. I confess I did dress in the bathroom when it was very cold, but then being comfortable is no harm in itself. The point was that I had air and space and could do things.

As to food, as far as I could see, people were healthy on all kinds of food not absolutely bad, if they had good digestion.

As to clothes, well, I can't stop here to *begin* to write what I thought about clothes as I was growing up, or what I think now. But as soon as I learned to sew I could see to it that mine did me no harm, anyhow. I even had some influence on Peggy's, but not much. Dear Peggy. She *is* so pretty, and so sweet. But I'm glad she has me to take care of her.

Well, I began very carefully. It was easy to get the idea from books, and to learn the dangers. The danger seemed to be mostly in straining oneself, overdoing it. Boys, of course, are always trying to stump one another, and as pleased as Punch when they can beat the other.

I hadn't anybody to get ahead of. I just wanted to *be* strong and limber and supple and skillful, not just to show it. And I wanted to build it in slowly, for keeps. So I began to do the exercises we had at school just a few minutes before I went to bed and when I got up.

They didn't amount to much. I soon invented more. It is so funny to me, the solemn way people talk about "systems" of physical culture. We've only got one kind of body, and there are only four limbs to it. One has trunk muscles, neck muscles, and arm and leg muscles, and there you are. One has nerves, too, and no amount of muscular strength is enough without nervous coordination.

Peggy and I played badminton in the attic. We had net shuttlecocks. Those parchment ones are too noisy. We made such a record that I got some of the boys interested and we had tournaments. It was pretty good fun for rainy days.

Then I started "graces," made some hoops and sticks from an old *Girls' Own Book* description. Peggy liked it, and so did other girls; the boys thought it was "sissyfied." We girls used to play in the yard on still days. It's awfully pretty.

Both Father and Mother disapproved of dancing, but running in that town was out of the question—for girls. But I said to myself, "Dancing is no mystery. I'll read about it." And I did.

I set to work in my attic, five minutes a day, ten minutes a day—a very little counts if you do it regularly. Such fun! I practiced the hardest steps I could find, and invented others, just as earnestly as I did things with my arms, and I'd recite poetry for music. It is merely keeping time, you see, and you can beat time to words as well as mere sounds.

"Horatius at the Bridge," that was a splendid dance, with marchings and posturings no end. Really "no end." It was so long I never could dance all through it.

"The Green, Green Gnome" was a beauty, so swift and light. Then there was my favorite "Songs of Seven." I made some lovely dances to go with that. It was really pretty work, too, and nobody knew about it. In the first place I had a good floor, and in the second place I made it my business from the very first to do it all like a pussycat—just moccasins, or barefoot, and coming down with the bent knee, never any jar. To dance like a Bacchante and make no noise, that was fun!

A big rope up over the rafters gave me all the arm work I wanted. One's own weight is enough to handle. I got so I could walk with my hands along a horizontal rope, or up and down one, just as easily. And so on, and so on.

Now that I'm eighteen and Mother wants me to be so proper, I sit and walk as quietly as anybody, but in my attic! Mother has no idea how far I can jump or how many times I can chin myself. The beauty of my plan is that I do what I want to, and never mention it. I feel like a happy miser.

All that is a solid success. I'm ever so strong and nobody knows it. As soon as I can I'm going to learn jujitsu too, and fencing.

But some three years ago I realized that bodies and brains aren't everything. What happened was this:

An old cousin of Father's came to see us. He had endless relatives in Scotland, but this one apparently had money enough to travel, and came over here. Father would have her with us, of course. She was a tall, stiff, rawboned old lady. I didn't like her a bit, especially as she criticized Mother right to her face, made a lot of extra work and care, and then found fault with her for doing it.

My general opinion was that the sooner she left the better, and I devoted my energies to getting rid of her. By lifting a board in my attic I found a place down in the side of the house, between the lath and plaster and the clapboards, and dropped a little arrangement on a string that made queer knockings in the night on her bedroom wall. On her windowpanes, hung invisibly from above, slow scratchings kept her awake. She'd open the window and look every way, but you can't see a black thread in the dark, especially when it only reaches the top pane. By daylight it wasn't there.

She was a superstitious old lady, and it scared her; also she was a suspicious old lady. She never found out that I had any hand in it, but she used to look at me queerly sometimes. I was too young then to seem as absolutely ordinary as I can now. Well, she left sooner than she meant to, and I was pleased.

In about two years that old lady died. She left Mother a legacy. Not Father, mind you, but Mother. And she left Peggy, dear, pretty sister Peggy, who hadn't been exceptionally polite, but had done a lot of little favors for "Mistress Feistonhaw," as Father called her (her name was Marget MacDougal Featherstonehaugh—an awful one), she left Peggy a set of cairngorms [smoky quartz]. They were beauties that had been in the family ever so long.

I didn't mind not getting anything half as much as I minded being mistaken. Here I'd thought she was horrid, blaming Mother so, and all the time she was sorry for her. If I had been too successful and had driven her away sooner, maybe it would have cost Mother that thousand pounds.

I may say right here that the money didn't do Mother any good. Father wanted it, of course, for one of his inventions. It was just the thing. It would save his life and make all our fortunes, and Mother couldn't refuse him anything. Pretty soon there was nothing left of Cousin Marget's legacy but the cairngorms and my lesson.

Here it is, in my secret diary:

"Wrong step. It is easy to be hateful and do mischievous tricks. It is harder to be kind and serviceable and *make friends*—but much wiser."

That was the beginning of my course of inside training, which I found even more fascinating than all the physical kind. There is only that little set of nerves and muscles to work with in physical culture, but once you begin on your mind there is no end to it.

It was tremendously exciting, this discovery—like being born and knowing it. So far I had just used the faculties I had to do things with and had been fairly successful. Then I had seen the necessity for health and strength—anybody can see that. In a year or two I had done wonders as quietly as could be.

Now it suddenly dawned on me that here was a field of growth beyond anything I had ever thought of before. I could improve my mental outfit. I was then about fifteen and a half. I can remember that day very well.

I went upstairs to my beloved garret, got out a big piece of paper, and began to set down the qualities I had and the qualities I hadn't, where what I had were weak and could be improved, or were undesirable and better left off, and the ones I wanted most that I needed in my business.

Here it is, again in my diary: "It is easier to do harm than to do good. Any small boy can do mischief—or girl, either. Doing good things is more difficult and therefore more interesting. Most of all you need to care for people, truly, so as to help them and to make friends. The more friends you have the more powerful you are!"

Then I considered the most popular people I knew and had read about. To my surprise I found that it was not by any means the best ones who were the best liked, nor even the ones who did the most for people. But certain qualities were attractive always.

They say the sculptor sees "the statue in the block." That's the way I felt. I began to *see* the kind of character I wanted, and, what's better, to see how to build it.

First of all, just as the main tool to work with, comes the power of one's own will over one's own body, *and* mind. The body part I had done a good deal on already, but now I invented a few more exercises, not for strength or skill, but merely for control.

But the mind part was such fun! For that matter it is yet, and as far as I can see it always will be.

Just look at your story books. Here's a man who kills another man—quite justifiably, maybe. All he has to do is to forget it and go about his business. But he can't forget it! He cannot keep the thought of it out of his mind. It haunts him, makes him miserable.

I can remember just how it was when I killed that kitten. Father was going to drown it, and he was so rough and horrid about it always. Of course, if you have a lady cat you do have kittens, and drowning is as easy as anything, I suppose. This was the one we always left for a while, for its mother's sake, and it got hurt, by a dog, I guess, and Father said he'd drown it.

I determined to chloroform it instead, so it would never know a thing or be scared. Doctor Branson gave me a little bottle and told me how to use it, and I got the poor thing asleep in my lap, and fixed the paper cone with some cloth in the point of it, and put it softly nearer and nearer her unsuspicious little nose. . . . I hate to think of that murder even now. How she did wiggle! I suppose some instinct warns them.

But I am sure it was easier for her than to be grabbed by Father, have a stone tied to her poor little neck, and be thrown, all wildly squirming, into cold water. I'm sure it was right to do. Then why should that unpleasant thing keep on agitating my mind?

So I practised on that. The moment it popped up into my consciousness, down it went quick, and I stood on the lid. In time I got quite rid of it. Almost everybody has some things they would rather not think of. Very well—don't, then. Self-control—active and passive—that is the first essential.

Then what? What *are* the best qualities, and which ones do people like the best? I had such a good time studying over a lot of biographies and asking questions of the other children. Half the time people do not know their own minds. They will tell you they approve of such and such qualities, but the people they like the best don't have them!

Of course, I know better now than I did at sixteen, and I dare say I shall know more when I'm twenty, but even as a girl I could see the facts in the case pretty fairly.

The most truly useful qualities are good sense, good will, courage and "power to act." But the qualities people like best are cheerfulness, politeness, and *taking an interest in them.* It's funny, people cannot abide anybody who is always talking about himself or herself. They call it selfish and self-centered, and self-conscious, and conceited and all sorts of hard names. But they dearly love the people who will smile intelligently, and listen and be interested while they talk about *them*selves.

This much I saw right away, and it did not take long to put it into practice. It must be done delicately and within reason, of course. People are suspicious of what they call flattery; it is an honest interest that they want, real sympathy, and to be understood.

Being understood. How we do ache for it. I wanted it,

too, when I was very young, but as soon as I really began to think about it I said, "Me understood? How *can* they? And if they did, then where would all my plans be?" So I put my foot on that little desire at once and fell to work trying to understand other people.

Good manners—that goes a long way. I read about those splendid old French noblemen and noblewomen being guillotined and not noticing it, and all sorts of stories of "high courtesy," and tried to imitate them. Then I ran up against something: people do not like your good manners to be conspicuously better than theirs. Sometimes it is good manners to use very poor ones, just to accommodate. Good manners that don't show, that was what I tried for, and I had several grades for use on different occasions. Not to get confused and betray myself, I analyzed them a little, and, after all, courtesy is just self-control and good will plus intelligence.

Cheerfulness was harder. Life was so deeply interesting to me and I worked so hard at it that I was inclined to glower a good deal. However, as soon as you've got your self-control going, you can acquire any characteristic you please—within reason.

I took Peggy for a pattern at first. Dear Mother was sweet and patient, but not cheerful. How could she be, having Father to put up with night and day? And *he* wasn't cheerful, dear knows. Neither was Alison.

It has taken me several years to get all these characteristics well in use, but I have. Peggy told me only yesterday that old Mrs. Watson told Mother she thought I had a "lovely character." I'm pleased, of course.

Well, one day I said to myself: "Come, here you are sixteen and over—all this training going on and nothing happening. Aren't there ever going to be any adventures?"

In books things happen. In life you have to make them happen. I decided I wanted to travel.

Travel for a young woman means visiting, and, generally, visiting relations. I knew I couldn't get to see Father's relations even if I wanted to. Mother's were all in Pennsylvania, and there we were up in Massachusetts.

Grandpa Chesterton lived on a big farm. His father had kept an inn and made a nice little fortune on it. Grandpa kept it, too, for a while. Then put his money with a real hotel in Philadelphia and got richer, then into a summer hotel by the ocean and got richer still. Then he sold them both and "retired."

There he was, on his big beautiful farm with plenty of money, and here was poor Mother having to beg and tease Father for every cent she got.

You see, Grandpa could not bear Father. (I don't wonder in the least.) He did not want Mother to marry him, and Mother just would, and did, and there we were.

At first Grandpa felt horribly about it, naturally. Then he sort of got over it and used to have us visit him, and Mother was foolish enough to persuade him to help Father in his schemes. But Father's schemes never came out right and Grandfather got angry all over again. Mother didn't say it like this, but this is what happened; I could make it out easily enough from what she said.

Grandpa hadn't been to see us, nor we to see him, since I was ten, though of course Mother wrote. He wouldn't ask Father there, and she wouldn't leave Father.

Then I began to write him letters—nice, simple, affectionate ones, but funny, too. I knitted him a pair of socks, just to show I could knit, and made him a blanket wrapper, to show I could sew. Grandpa was a widower, you see, and even if he was rich he liked to have people think of him.

And I made him some jelly—the kind he liked best. I wrote a letter on purpose to ask him. And once, a particular kind of fruitcake Mother had the recipe of. You can't buy it.

When it came vacationtime, I asked Grandpa if I mightn't come and visit him. I said Mother was pretty well, and Peggy could help her at home, and I had saved all I had for the trip; that I was quite grown up now and it would only take one day, starting early. I said I was afraid Father wouldn't like it, but that I hadn't asked him yet, and maybe he wouldn't let me.

That annoyed Grandpa, I think. Anyway, he said he should like nothing better than a visit from his industrious granddaughter, and sent me a ticket with careful directions, and told where he would meet me in New York. This seemed a pity, but I should at least have half the trip by myself, and *something* might happen.

The real adventure was in getting started. Father never would consent to it, I knew, but it is one thing to refuse to allow a person to go and another to get them back again. I was sorry for Mother, too. Father would blame her, of course, but I had been so careful all winter, so good and so *ordinary* that I felt as if I should explode if something didn't happen.

This wasn't disobedience, for no one had forbidden me to go. It was just enterprising. I packed all I needed in a flat brown paper package and added to it some stuff we had to change at the store. It wasn't going to be a long visit, that was pretty sure. I did not have to take much.

After Father had gone downtown I trotted off, not telling Mother, because if she didn't know, Father couldn't scold her quite so much. I didn't sneak. I told Mother I was going to change that gingham at Browning's. I was and I did. Lying is not necessary. I always tell the truth—when I tell anything— nothing but the truth. As to telling the whole truth, nobody *can* do that—we don't know it.

Then I mailed a note that she'd get before dinner telling her all about it, and that I'd slipped off so as not to have to tease Father. I sent her Grandpa's letter and all, and told her I would let Father know downtown. I did. He got my letter by the last mail and was displeased, of course. That was to be expected. But by the time he got his letter I was in New York with Grandpa.

But the best fun was my own journey alone. I had been over the road before, as a child, and had plenty of directions, but it was exciting, all the same. So much of my life was *inside*, so many of the things I did I had to keep to myself, and behaving *just so* to all the people about me was still so much of an effort that it was just magnificent to be At Large. It *rested me*—miles of me.

I am not pretty nor in any way conspicuous. Sort of mouse-brown hair, bluish eyes. (I always wished I'd had the Italian eyes, but Peggy got those. Mine were Scotch.) A healthy-looking young woman—who wouldn't be with all the training I've done?—but not especially attractive.

The compliments I've had are from old ladies and gentlemen and not very many of them, but they please me. I am "quiet" and "well mannered" and "always pleasant," they say.

I sat there in the car with my bundle and little shopping bag, holding my ticket, and looking like any young woman going somewhere, but I felt like Balboa.

Crowds of people got in. A big woman tried to sit down by me, and I politely got up and gave her the window. Then I was able to get out when I wanted to. Some people were pigs—took two seats, facing, and filled them with bundles. A little woman with a child and a baby couldn't find a place and had to sit on the square-backed end seat and hold them both.

When the conductor came through I asked him if there wouldn't be room for that little woman with the baby in front of me where two women were taking up more than their share of the seats. Conductors are generally nice to women with babies, and I suppose they have their troubles with the piggy kind often enough. He scowled a little, went and spoke to the baby woman, brought her back, and piled the baggage of the other two up over their heads and under their feet. They had to sit together then, and wished they hadn't turned the other seat over, I guess. Small children are tiresome neighbors sometimes.

By and by I borrowed the baby. I like babies and they like me, and this was a jolly one. The big woman beside me had gorgeous clothes and she didn't seem to fancy having the child touch her.

"Isn't he a dear?" I said, smiling up into her face. But as soon as there was another seat vacant she squeezed out and took it. I made a mental note for future use: "When you don't like your seatmate, borrow a baby."

Then the baby began to play peekaboo with his sister between the heads of the two woman in front of me, and by and by they changed, too, getting the brakeman to take their baggage. Then I slipped into their seat, and the baby went to sleep with his mother and the little girl with me. It was a real family scene.

But she got out, more people came in, the seat was turned again, and then a man came and sat by me. I didn't like him at all. His breath was like Father's, but more tobaccoey. His clothes were too showy. He had big rings, and a big watch chain and a big scarf pin. He looked me over a while, and then spoke to me. I felt a real thrill. This was going to be an adventure, I hoped.

"Traveling alone, miss?" he asked.

Anybody could see I was, but I said, "Yes."

"Going far?"

"To New York," I answered.

I could see him meditating on that, and I didn't like the way he meditated. He looked The Villain in books. I had so wanted to meet a Villain!

"Going to your folks?" he asked in a very friendly voice—too friendly.

"I've left home," I said, and drew myself up a little and turned my face away. But I could see him, for he leaned forward with his arm on the back of the seat in front of us and looked me over.

"Got friends living in New York?" he next inquired.

"No," I said, rather reluctantly.

He sat back at that, pulled his waistcoat down, thought a minute and then made some general remarks about "the big city."

Presently he asked if I was expecting to get work in New York. I said I hoped to. I did; always had, do yet. Some day I will.

"Do you know what hotel you're going to?" was his next question.

"I can ask a policeman, can't I?" I said, looking up at him.

"Don't ask anything of a New York policeman," he said heartily. "Just you trust to me, young lady. I'll take you to a nice hotel."

"I don't want an expensive one," I said carefully, and he chuckled over that.

"Oh, no," he said, "not an expensive one."

Grandpa's letter had said "Give your bag to a porter and come to the ladies' waiting room. I will be there near the restroom. If we miss each other tell the matron and wait there. That is safer than by the gate."

I had no bag and wouldn't let the man take my little bundle, but I told him I had to go to the ladies' room first, and he trotted right along and said he'd wait for me.

Oh, it was fine—just splendid. Even if Grandpa hadn't been there, I knew there was a woman who took care of young women traveling alone, and I'd tell her. But Grandpa was there, and he's a big, strong old man and has a temper, even if he is a Quaker.

I told The Villain to wait a minute, I'd be right back, and I was—with Grandpa. Grandpa collared him and dragged him to a big policeman, though he struggled awfully.

I'd afraid he did not spend the night in that nice hotel.

ც~ # CHAPTER FIVE

Grandpa was pleased to see me, I think, but got very angry about that man. I did not tell him how he had sat by me and talked. I just said, "He got out with me and would carry my bag." That was true. And I began to ask Grandpa questions about the farm so as to take up his mind.

"I can't stay long," I said. "Mother was glad to have me come, I'm sure, but I didn't dare tell Father until to-day. I'm afraid I'm very naughty, Grandfather, but I just . . . left word for Father. I knew he'd stop me if I asked, and I had the ticket, and I did want to come so. Are you angry with me?"

He tried to tell me that it was wrong to come away like that, and I was very meek about it.

"I can't say I'm sorry, though," I told him, "because really I'm glad! But Father'll be sure to write for me to come back at once. And you'll have to read it, and then I'll have to go right home. . . .

"Never mind. Tell me about the cows, Grandfather, and

the white-tiled stalls, and the white clothes of the dairymen, and everything."

I had been reading up about model dairy farms. I read somewhere that Edward Everett Hale said if anybody would spend one winter reading up on any chosen subject they would know more about it than anybody else except the great specialists.

I'd never given a whole winter to anything yet, but I'd found this (our librarian had helped me to it): if you want to know something about something quick, you go to the most recent encyclopedia and get your outline; then you look up some of the books mentioned and you finish with *Poole's Index*—get the very latest articles in the technical magazines. In a day or two you can learn lots and lots, especially if you know how to pick out the most important things, not clutter up your mind with too many details. The librarian showed me that part. Seems to me they ought to teach us that in school.

Well, I had quite a fund about Grandpa's subjects, and I chattered some and listened more, and asked him if he'd seen the article about Lord Esterville's new farm in *The Country Leader,* or if he'd read Mr. Brushe's book on milk. That man is a doctor, a veterinarian *and* a dairyman—he ought to know. This was while we were on the train going to Philadelphia, and while we stopped at Trenton I saw a telegraph boy coming through the car calling "Chesterton! Chesterton!" Grandpa had stepped out to get a paper, so I said to the boy, "It's for my grandfather. He'll be back in a minute. It is expected." I had had a dreadful feeling that Father would telegraph, but I never dreamed he'd do it on the train, never knew anybody could. So the boy skipped off, and Grandpa came back, but the telegram was in my pocket.

I had peeked at the name at the end, but I didn't read it. I didn't mean to. As for Grandpa, he could honestly say that he never got the telegram. He never did.

I breathed a little easier then. They'd expect me back right away, and would get my letter instead. I wrote a nice one to Father, telling what a nice time I was having and how grateful I was, just as if he'd sent me with his blessing; and a card to

Mother, too, telling her I'd written to Father, that Grandpa met me all right and everything was lovely. Then they'd write, of course, but I should at least have been there.

On the other train I was pretty still. Grandpa asked me if I was tired, but I said no, it wasn't that. Was I homesick already? "Oh, no!" I said. "No, indeed, but I was afraid that . . . Tell me, has a grandfather any rights?"

"What do you mean, child?" he asked.

"Why, Mother is glad to have me come—she'd come herself, you know, only—only. . ."

"I know," he said grimly, nodding his head.

"And I'm as glad as can be to come, to see you and the wonderful farm, but suppose Father shouldn't like it a bit? Sometimes Father is a little . . . well, he doesn't seem to realize how much other people want a thing. Suppose he wrote that you must send me right back. Would you have to do what he told you?"

Grandpa set his jaw. He had a big, quiet face, a lot of strong gray hair, eyes that looked as if they'd like to be fierce, but with the little wrinkles around them that laughing makes.

"I'll send you home in good order," he said, "and in good time. Don't you worry about that."

I didn't, any more.

Mother told me afterwards that Father wrote a very peremptory letter, very peremptory indeed. He told her all about it, and she cried and tried to make him not send it. But he did.

They were looking for me the next day, in answer to the telegram, it appeared, and I didn't come, and then he wrote.

Meanwhile I'd given Grandpa the big handkerchief I'd initialed for him, and he'd taken me all over the farm, and we'd had a long ride over the place and around it and had a real nice evening together. I sat on a little stool by his knee, and asked him to tell me things about when he was a boy, and about his mother, when she was a little girl, and we got on beautifully.

Next morning I was up early and got all the morning mail and brought it in. Sure enough there was that letter.

I gave Grandpa all the others first, and then slowly brought that one out.

"Here it is," I said. "And you'll have to read it—and it'll say to send me back *at once*, and I'll have to go."

Grandpa turned it over in his hand and studied it a while.

"It's your father's writing, and I dare say you are correct as to what he says, but as to having to read it, I do not know of any law that compels a man to read his letters until he gets ready to. I can answer it," he went on, a slow smile crinkling around the corners of his eyes, "without reading it."

Mother told me about that, too, long afterward. Father was so enraged that he shook it in her face, made her read it, and blamed her for the whole thing.

Grandpa acknowledged his "favor postmarked the 14th," said he had not yet found time to read it, and went on to tell what an extremely pleasant visit he was having with me.

Of course, Father answered furiously, got no reply to that, and then made Mother write. She was frightened and worried, but Grandpa wrote her a letter saying that I was perfectly well and happy and in safe hands. He added, "If her father disinherits her, I will not." That quieted Father some.

I learned a lot at Grandpa's.

Having already picked up a good bit of the theory of dairy farming, I was immensely interested and studied the practical workings with real enthusiasm. I was up early to watch the milking, and Grandpa let me learn to milk on an unimportant cow they kept for their own use. She was just as good as the others, but they weren't watching her record so religiously.

So I milked assiduously, morning and night. You never know when a thing like that is going to be useful.

I watched the dairymen. The real difficulty, Grandpa told me, was with them. There had to be a good many of them, young fellows mostly, and they simply would not be as careful as they ought to.

"Do they earn much?" I asked.

"More than they deserve," he said, and gruffly, too. I saw that there were limits to the legitimate curiosity of granddaughters. But I learned all he told me and a good deal more.

And I studied Grandpa assiduously. (I like that word. It seems to stick right *to* a thing, and shake it.) I tried to think of something I could do for him, but beyond small services and presents there wasn't anything to do. He had plenty of money. He had plenty of occupation. He had plenty of servants to wait on him. And he had a housekeeper—a fine one.

She was a big, handsome woman, very efficient, with smooth, pleasant manners, but I could feel at once that she didn't like me. Now, why shouldn't she? I'd never done her any harm, and I wasn't staying long enough to alienate Grandpa's affections, as they call it. She was polite enough—more than I liked; but I was just as polite as she was.

All at once I remembered. Of course. She wanted to marry Grandpa. Wasn't he a widower, and rich, and old, and alone? That is, with no real family of his own to love and do for?

In the books I had read there were many of these housekeepers—very designing persons, and sometimes successful.

I studied the situation carefully. What could I do? If it was so, what on earth could I do?

Maybe she didn't want to marry him after all. I looked at her, and I looked at him, and studied about it. Of course, I didn't look as if I was studying.

She was not the oily kind of villain you read about, just calm and interested and agreeable. I made up my mind to find out if that was her natural manner, or put on.

It was not hard to make friends with her. She was being as friendly as could be to me, and I stayed with her quite a little when Grandpa was busy.

Her housekeeping was admirable. I admired it warmly, praised her preserves—which were really praiseworthy—and her way of managing everything. She showed me about, showed me the linen closet and the cedar closet and cedar chests. I guessed she wanted me to be impressed and tell Grandpa. I was impressed, and said so, too, right in front of her. But I also got very friendly with the maids, as far as I could. There was a new one, a chambermaid who did my room, and I found that she was awfully afraid of Mrs. Mason, the housekeeper, that she was very strict and harsh with them. That wouldn't appeal to Grandpa as any harm—he liked discipline. Gerta was a Swede—the chambermaid, I mean. The parlor maid was German. It took a lot of people to keep that big house in order.

Gerta was very pretty, and very lonesome and homesick, poor dear. She had no end of admirers, though, not only the dairymen and farmhands, but the tradesmen who came driving up in their joggly little carts. And she used to tell me about it, what they said and did, having no one else to confide in. She didn't like the German one, or the cook, who was English. She said they didn't like her, either.

One day she was feeling dreadful because Mrs. Mason had scolded her for flirting with the dairy foreman, and she confided her feelings to me. Of course I encouraged it, or she wouldn't have dared. She said Mrs. Mason was so severe with them all, and so hard on them if they did any little thing, that she threatened to send her away without a character reference if she caught her alone with any of the men again.

"She said, 'You Swedes are all alike!' " sobbed Gerta. "She may scold me, but not my country! And she is not so good herself. I know that!"

I wondered what Gerta knew, and set myself to find out. It was not very difficult; she was angry and miserable enough to tell me anything for a little kindness. I comforted her all I could (she seemed younger than I was, though really older in years), told her I knew she was a good girl, and had perfect confidence in her. I had. I could see just the kind of a person she was—the victim kind: good, but childish and weak, not using her brains at all.

Well, it appeared that one of the young butcher men had resented Mrs. Mason's snapping at him for joking with Gerta, and had told Gerta, afterward, that "the Old Lady" had better be careful how she pitched into him, that he could "take her down a peg" if he wanted to tell all he knew.

I told Gerta that it was her duty to her employer to find out about it, that Mrs. Mason was only an employee, and that if Mrs. Mason was doing anything she shouldn't, Grandpa ought to know it. Then I represented to her what fun it would be to have a sort of stick to hold over her—even if we never told—and then I said I didn't feel sure the young butcher man really knew anything, or that he would tell her if he did.

Gerta tossed her head at that, and a very decided sparkle came into her clear blue eyes. She had such a peachy complexion. And her neck was round and straight as . . . well, in the books they say "an alabaster column," but hers was so soft and cuddly that it didn't remind me of a column at all, nor yet of alabaster.

I teased her a little more and she just said, "You shall see, Miss MacAvelly," and went off to make more beds, as we heard Mrs. Mason's foot on the stairs.

Gerta was a very determined person when she made up her mind. She began to encourage not only the butcher, but the baker and the . . . I want to say "candlestick maker," but it was only the grocer, and one and all of them told the same story.

"She hass a 'rake-off,' Miss MacAvelly—that iss what they call it. There go large bills to Mr. Chesterton, and not all of it is to the tradesmen. She does all the ordering, and gets her 'ten percent off,' but Mr. Chesterton does not get it—not at all."

Now, this was something worthwhile. I felt as Machiavellian as could be, and wondered how I could get the facts and prove it to Grandpa.

For once I was helped by Fate. Fate is not very dependable as an assistant, and is quite apt to work the wrong way. But this time it happened beautifully.

It appeared Mrs. Mason had a son. She always represented him as a most noble young man, but I had my doubts of that. Anyway, this son was sick in a hospital, and she had to go to him.

I was all sympathy and told Grandpa that he could let her go as easily as not, that I'd keep house for him; I had done it at home and knew how.

He hadn't much confidence in me, I guess, but the cook was a dependable woman, and Mrs. Mason said she would be back in a few days—a week at most, she thought.

He let me try. There really was nothing else to do. It

surely wasn't worthwhile to get a new housekeeper just for a week.

Off went Mrs. Mason on a Saturday, in real distress. I was quite sorry for her. No woman wants her son to be sick, no matter what her own designs may be. Whether she was that kind of a "designing woman" I don't know—and as a matter of fact I never did find out—but that she was cheating Grandpa was clear enough.

I spent Saturday evening studying cookbooks and menus; Sunday, the market reports; and started out early Monday morning to see all those tradesmen. Grandpa was much amused at my businesslike airs.

He let me have the buggy with the old mare, and a good deal older man to drive me about, one who knew the people we traded with. It was lucky that I'd been about a good deal already, and picked up some information, now I was in a position to use it.

It had not taken long to run over the supplies in the house; the cook helped me do that. She was a very competent sort of person, and I had shown great respect for her ability without treating her as an equal. I learned about that from our Alison. She had worked for fine English families, and had always had a good deal to say about their manners, and how superior they were to ours in America.

There was a lot of food on hand, stored away, and yet Mrs. Mason had kept buying and buying. I determined to keep all my accounts separate, and asked Grandpa to let me pay cash for the week, so as not to confuse the accounts. So he made an estimate from a number of the monthly bills and gave me a quarter of their average amount.

Then I used all the intelligence and experience I had, as well as a disarming expression of childlike confidence. I had the catalog of the biggest grocer in the town where we traded, and a list of things—quite a good-sized one, because there were a lot of us to feed. With the list and the prices, I asked the principal man in the store if he would give me a cash discount if I ordered all my groceries there, in weekly supplies like this.

I showed him the money all ready, told him my name was

MacAvelly, that I was newly come to the place, and was being allowed to try my hand as housekeeper, and that I wanted to show how much I could save. He never realized that it was the Chesterton account until he agreed to make the discount I asked. Then he inquired about Mrs. Mason and I told him she had left rather suddenly.

I didn't tell him why, nor that she was expected to be back, just tightened my mouth a little and said my grandfather was letting me try, and I was considering where to place our trade.

He looked at me a little queerly, seemed to realize that a small honest bird in the hand was worth a dishonest cassowary in the bush, and said he hoped I would make no change, that he was sure I should find everything satisfactory. I told him I was sure of it, with a confiding smile, and skipped out. There was singularly little trouble with the tradesmen.

Of course we raised our own vegetables—lovely fresh ones, of all sorts and kinds; and we had our own milk and eggs and chickens. The eggs, Grandpa said, did not pay very well, but I had a shrewd suspicion as to the reason.

The man who had charge of the hennery was very friendly with Mrs. Mason, and I felt sure there was a leak there. He had showed me all over the place in the first day or two of my visit, showed me the nests, and even told me how many hens were laying. Since then he had been at some pains to explain that they were not laying at all regularly, and there were certainly not enough, after our family consumption, to suit Grandpa's ideas of profit.

I made a special study of that hennery—hen's eggs are golden eggs to the producer. Then I asked Grandpa if he would do me a favor—just one.

"What now, young lady?" he demanded. "Housekeeping money gone already?" It was only Wednesday.

"Oh no," I said. "The housekeeping's getting along all right, and I do hope you like the meals, Grandfather."

"They do very well," said Grandpa. He did not believe

in praising people overmuch. I didn't mind what he *said* about the meals. I'd seen him eat them.

"This is something very particular," I told him. "You know I've kept hens at home, and made them pay too. I really do know quite a lot about them. And I think it's funny, really very funny, that you don't get more eggs. Now will you let me collect them, for just one day? Send Joe Farrel on some errand or other, make him take a day off. I can attend to everything for one day—the incubators and chicks and all."

Grandpa put down his paper and looked at me severely. "Do you mean to say you think Joe Farrel is dishonest?"

"I don't know, Grandfather, and I can't tell until I count the eggs myself, but so many hens, on the proper food, at this time of year, ought to produce about so many eggs" (I forget now what the number was, but then I had it all worked out). "And they don't, not by a good thirty percent."

He looked at my figures. I had the books there to show him, and the poultry journal, and he nodded his big head slowly up and down.

"You take a very lively interest in affairs, for so young a person," he said, looking at me almost disapprovingly.

"I guess it's because I am so young, Grandfather. You see, all this is fresh to me, and I'm, well, I suppose I am proud of the way I worked my little hennery." I was. It always gave me pleasure to recall how many more eggs I had than there were hens.

"Of course I'm only a beginner at housekeeping, but I did it all the summer Mother was so poorly, and she said I did as well as she herself." Really I did it better, a lot better, but I never told her so, nor yet Grandpa.

After a while he agreed to send Farrel away on a sudden errand, told him he'd be responsible for the hens for one day, and I had my chance.

The hens were all right. There were three dozen more eggs than the day before—thirty-eight, to be exact. I was awfully pleased. Grandpa wasn't. He sent Farrel off again, for another day, and the hens kept up the record. Then the man returned, nothing being said, and he seemed to have a most discouraging influence on those birds.

Well, he was fired pretty quick, and a new man found that "knew not Joseph"—that is, Mrs. Mason. Farrel was mean enough to accuse her of putting him up to it, and sharing the profit, but Grandpa didn't believe him. I didn't say anything—not yet—but "kept house" for all I was worth.

She didn't come back at the end of the week. She sent word that her son was worse, asked for two weeks, and hoped we were getting along all right under "the young lady's care."

We were. We got along beautifully. Gerta tried to be lazy, to take advantage of our previous friendliness. I told her I was a real professional now, that I meant to be nice to all of them, but she'd have to do her work, not only as well, but quite a bit better than she did before—and I showed her how.

You see my mother was an Exquisite Housekeeper—not a Good Business Manager, not at all—but as a Work Manager she was fine.

Grandpa began to look very appreciative.

"The place seems more as it used to when your mother was with me," he said, "and your grandmother. You look like her, a little."

I don't really believe I did a single bit, but he thought so. And if I didn't look like her, I'm sure the things he had to eat looked like what he used to have, and tasted so too. I had brought Mother's old recipe book with me—the little hand-written one that was her mother's—and when the solemn English cook wouldn't undertake a thing, I just made it myself.

There were popovers—she had never seen or heard of popovers. And there was real sponge cake—all eggs, no baking powder; and real pound cake—pound o' butter, pound o' sugar, pound o' flour, and a dozen eggs.

The most Pennsylvanianish things he had had right along, but they seemed to please him better now. And I made some sweet pickle, the green tomato kind. He smiled all over his face that night.

"You certainly know how to cook, Benigna," he said, as pleased as could be. "You take after your mother and your grandmother too. I don't begrudge you the housekeeping, my dear, no matter what it costs."

That was a lot for Grandpa to say, and it pleased me ever so much—just to succeed like that, to say nothing of what else I was trying to do.

I kept account of the eggs we used, the milk we used, and the butter—all the stuff of the farm—and found that I was getting on with less. I had a real square talk with the cook about it.

"I know I am young, Mrs. Owens," I said, "and you have had far more experience, but I will give you a dollar a week extra out of the housekeeping money, if you will help me save it."

She was a desperately saving person—in money, I mean—had some family dependent on her, I imagined, though she never said so, and this pleased her. There was almost a gleam in her large dull eyes, but all she said was "Certainly, Miss."

Meanwhile Mrs. Mason's son failed to recover, and she failed to come back, and kept on writing letters and begging for one week more. Grandpa wrote to her to take all the time she wanted, until it was more than a month later.

At the end of that time I brought Grandpa my accounts. He was sitting by the big library table with the droplight, reading a book about the dairy industry in Denmark, when I came and stood quietly, with the account book, and the price lists, and all.

"What is it, my dear?" he asked, looking at me so pleasantly that it made me think of Mother. We'd had a *lovely* supper that night.

I asked if I might interrupt him long enough to "give an account of my stewardship," and he smiled and made room by his chair for me. Then I showed him all that I'd bought, what I'd paid for it, and that I had a good quarter of the money he'd given me left over.

"What's this?" he said.

"What I've saved," I answered proudly. He knew how well we'd lived, too. Then he got out the old accounts and looked at them.

"How do you explain the difference, child?" he asked.

I told him I paid cash, in quantity, with one delivery a week—that saved some. That I had bought only what was needed—that saved more. "The closets are full of extra stuff," I told him, "and some of it is spoiled."

"But twenty-five percent," he said. "A whole quarter of the table expenses!"

I said I was not sure—could not be—but that one of the maids *thought* . . . and so on.

Then he called in Gerta and questioned her until she cried, but she stood her ground and told him what the market boys had said—all of them.

Grandpa was awfully angry.

It was no use for me to try to placate him and say I understood it was frequently done—just a sort of commission for patronage. He has very strict views about honesty, my grandfather has.

Mrs. Mason never came back.

CHAPTER SIX

Peggy wrote me that Mother was sick again, and I went home in a hurry.

Father was much too worried then to be as angry with me as he would have been otherwise. He needed me. When Mother was really sick in bed and had the doctor, then Father used to feel badly—at least he acted so.

As I grow older I am beginning to make allowances for people, to see that they do have double natures or triple or more so, and probably Father thinks that he "loves" Mother. I heard him once, talking solemn Scotch religion and morality to a Presbyterian minister out on the veranda. They sat and smoked and discussed doctrines, and argued over texts, and finally they got onto what the minister called "the sins of the flesh." (I used to think that meant diseases—it ought to.) The minister was inclined to be a little lenient, but not Father.

"A man must keep the law!" he said. "There is no excuse for any sin. A man must leave father and mother and cleave to his wife. I have done so. I have always been true to Benigna."

Well, if being true means sticking to her, he certainly had. But it seemed to me that Mother would have been better off if he had . . . prevaricated a little.

Dr. Bronson was worried; I could see that. He had known Mother so long, and he seemed really interested.

"She must go away," he told Father. "She needs a change, and rest—perfect rest."

She did; even I could see that. But she didn't go; she just sat around, pale and weak, and tired-looking, and I ran the house. It didn't seem anything, after Grandpa's.

The doctor told her she must have a separate room and sleep more, but she never dared mention it but once. Father was furious.

"He'll interfere between a man and his wife, will he?" he said. "We'll have a doctor who knows the laws of decency better than that!" And Mother dropped the subject. She couldn't bear to think of losing Dr. Bronson.

When Father scolded at Mother, which was often, I could hear in my attic because there was a stovepipe hole that was used to warm the place when they had stoves. It was covered now with a piece of tin, but tin doesn't shut out sound much.

Besides, I fixed it so it would turn—just took out a nail or two and moved it sideways. I never could see why people are so fierce about listening. It doesn't say in the Bible "Thou shalt not listen." I looked, with a concordance. And there's no law against it. You have to find out things somehow, especially if you're handicapped by not telling lies.

I suppose really that my great Italian ancestor told lies like anything, but I can't somehow. Too much Scotch Presbyterian and Quaker, I suppose.

When Mother was fairly well again—as well as she ever was, poor dear—I began to worry about Peggy.

Peggy was about as sweet and nice a child as ever was, but Father thwarted her so she just had to do something. She had an idea she wanted to go to college, but he set his foot down hard on that. College was no place for a woman, no daughter of his should be seen in such a place, and so on. So she had to give up that ambition. An ambition is a great deal of company—wholesome, too, I think.

Next she set her heart on music. They said she had a voice. Somebody encouraged her, and she quite blossomed out again, and wanted to take lessons and even go abroad—maybe!

That idea fared no better than the other. He said he had no money to waste on such foolishness, that the place for girls was at home, that a wife need not be an opera singer—all sorts of things like that. She could sing ballads to him in the evenings quite well enough, he said, no more was necessary.

Well, Peggy took to reading novels. I didn't wonder. If you can't do things yourself you have to get interested in other people's doing them.

And then Father must cut off the novels—as far as he could. She did read some, surreptitiously, but they were no longer a real resource.

So of course I wasn't surprised when she began to take an interest in boys, because Peggy's a bit older than I am, and twice as pretty. And then it was worse than ever. It was bad enough to have Father looking as he did and always around, enough to drive anybody away. But Peggy was so pretty and Mother was so sweet (she loved boys; she'd have liked a houseful of them, and was always sorry she had none of her own) that they would come. Then when they asked Peggy to go anywhere, Father always refused. Always. Party, sleigh ride, skating, going to walk—anything with a young man, it made no difference, he'd forbid it. And he'd talk about it for days, as if Peggy were planning to elope with these fellows. She would blush way up to the little pale gold fuzzes around the edges of her hair, and cry, and I got so angry that I felt like being a man and calling Father out for insulting my sister.

Of course after a little she never asked to go, and tried to keep the boys away. But they would come. They'd walk home from school with her, and come to the fence down at the corner of the garden where the alley touched our place, and things like that. Father just made a business of watching Peggy and surprising her with some nice fellow. And then the things he'd say to that young man, and to her!

Well, I knew what the result would be well enough. That is as clear as daylight in most any story. A girl with a father like that, and no freedom or pleasure in her life, always rushes off and marries the wrong man. Her whole life is ruined, just by having a mean father!

I remember one morning at breakfast—it was the first of the month and a lot of bills came all together. Father did about as mean a thing as I ever saw or read of. At least he tried to.

Mother was wretched. She had a headache, hadn't slept any, she said. I knew she hadn't slept much, for I'd been awakened over and over, and Father was holding forth every time.

He sat there and opened all the bills, and found fault with them. Said we were careless in the housekeeping, that Mother could keep accounts no better than a child of ten, that we were extravagant.

"Look at this meat bill!" he said. "Thirty-six dollars for meat alone! It is scandalous, woman!"

"It is for three months, Angus!" said Mother. "It has not been paid. Bills don't grow smaller by neglect."

"No," said he, "they grow larger by neglect—'tis that I am complaining of! It is care that makes them small. Intelligent care and supervision and economy. You were brought up in a loose public house where the money flowed like water—all out and none in, I may add!"

"If little came in it was because the whiskey did *not* flow like water!" cried Mother. She never could stand it to have him pitch on Grandpa. Besides, Grandpa made money enough, in time.

A dark red crept up to Father's hair, which was red, too, but not so dark, and he looked around for a weapon. I don't mean a carving knife or a poker, but for some especially mean thing to say.

The letters were all under his hand; he always made Alison bring them to him first. Peggy used to get her letters—particular ones—sent to her friend Jenny Gale sometimes, but this time by some mistake there was one for her from Ned Wallace, right under Father's hand. It even had the name printed on the corner—one of his father's office envelopes. Ned was a new one and hadn't learned how things were with us. He was Peggy's richest admirer, but I liked him the least of all. I don't think she cared much for him really, but felt rather vain of his attentions. He had a bad reputation—they said he was very fast, had had to leave college in disgrace, and that's why his parents sent him abroad.

And now here was Father, ugly as could be, holding this letter in his hand. That was a weapon indeed.

"Aha!" he said. "Now we shall have a little entertainment."

Peggy looked frightened and desperate. Mother saw what he had and how Peggy looked, and she got very white.

"You aren't going to read my letter!" cried poor Peggy.

"Would you insinuate that your father was not a gentleman?" he asked her. "Should I read another person's letters, like a meddlesome woman? By no means, Miss Margaret MacAvelly. But you are going to read the letter—aloud."

He handed it to her.

"Read the letter. It will doubtless be very amusing," he went on. "Let us hear what your friend, Mr. Wallace, has to say. Is he the elegant young clothes-horse I found you walking with last week, in disobedience to my express commands?"

"No, I can't!" said Peggy, and held her letter tight.

"We will now see the virtue of obedience, as developed by the kindergarten method," said Father to poor Mother. "You will observe, madam, how your efforts at child culture have fared."

Peggy looked desperately at Mother and Mother began to straighten up and catch her breath. She was going to say something that I knew would make it worse—when the bell rang. I started to go to the door, with other plans in view, but Father took me by the elbow and sat me down again.

"Sit down!" he said. "You have not been excused. We are not through with our breakfast, let alone our letters. Alison McNab will go to the door."

Which Alison did, announcing a gentleman to see Father.

"Show him in here," Father said. "We shall not be interrupted in our meals." And in came Billy Anderson.

Peggy gave a little gasp—she couldn't help it. But I just

looked once at him, a sort of sharp warning look, and then at my plate. Billy was an old schoolmate of ours, and had always hung around after Peggy, but I think she didn't value him much. He was an ordinary sort of boy, and when he left school rather early to go to work she hadn't missed him; there were plenty of more attractive fellows.

Well, Father saw the jump Peggy gave and he turned around in his chair and looked the boy over. He remembered him, too. Billy used to walk home from school with Peggy—persistently.

"It is rather early, is it not, to call upon young ladies?" he asked.

Bill felt that he was not exactly *persona grata,* I guess.

"Excuse me, Mr. MacAvelly," he said. "I am pleased to see Mrs. MacAvelly and your daughters" (with a little bow), "but my business is with you."

"And what is your business with me, young man?" demanded Father. "State your business at once, if you please."

Then Billy, with evident reluctance, had to say that he called about Bliss & Company's bill, as they had put the matter in the hands of his agency to collect.

I had heard that his last job was with a bill collecting agency, but I never thought he'd come collecting bills from Father!

I can't remember all Father said, but I did admire Billy. He kept his temper perfectly, made a little compliment to Mother, and got in a reassuring smile at Peggy. Father showed him the door, but he got out with undisturbed dignity, and left the bill.

Then Father returned to the charge, angrier than ever.

"I admire your taste in suitors!" he said to Peggy, "and your suitor's taste in occupation. To dun on one's own account is despicable enough, but to make a business of hounding gentlemen in their own homes on other men's accounts—getting a paltry commission, I've no doubt—making a beggarly living out of the temporary embarrassments of their betters—'tis a cross between a bailiff and a jackal! Will you ring the bell for some hot coffee, madam? And now let us hear that letter!"

Peggy didn't know how to get out of it. She wasn't a bit

inventive. Mother tried to shield her, but Father turned on her with such cutting and disagreeable words that she grew frantic in her helplessness, and was rising from her chair to do I don't know what when Alison came in with the coffee.

Then I jumped up and took it from her, turned to set it by Mother, caught my foot on something and stumbled. The coffee went all across the table. Father pushed back his chair to avoid the floor. "You awkward gowk!" he cried.

Peggy jumped up with a scream.

"Are you hurt, Peggy?" I cried, running to her, and began to wipe off the coffee with my napkin, getting the letter away from her as I did so.

Mother had dropped into her chair. I thought she'd faint. And Alison came running to clear up things.

Then I slipped out through the gate to get Dr. Bronson, who lived close by. I told him he must come quick. And it was time somebody came, for Father was storming at Peggy and Mother was standing between them. Of course it stopped as soon as Dr. Bronson came in. I told him about the accident and he looked at Peggy's hand, but more at Mother, and Father concluded to go downtown.

Mother was hysterical and, well, queer. The doctor insisted that she should go to bed and gave her bromide. When he came down I was waiting for him.

"Doctor," I said, "What is the matter with Mother? Why doesn't she get better? Isn't there *anything* we can do?"

He stood looking at me, pulling on his gloves. "Your mother must go away," he said. "*Must,* if she is to get back her strength."

"Father won't let her," I said. "There isn't any money. She won't leave us. She told me it was no use, when you said that last summer, that she might as well die here as anywhere!"

"Look here, Benigna," he said, "I've known you since you were a baby, and you have a good head for a child. Now you and Peggy must get your mother away. She cannot stand this much longer. I have spoken to your father about it. She must have quiet, plenty of sleep, rest, and relief from all anxiety and irritation." And off he went. It's easy for doctors to say what you must do.

Father had set his foot down that it was all nonsense—that a woman's place was at home—that nothing ailed Mother but "nerves," which last was true enough—it wasn't muscles, nor bones.

I went down to the end of the garden that afternoon to think it out. There was a sort of little summerhouse on the lowest terrace, well shaded, right near the fence, and there was Peggy talking to Ned Wallace! Peggy was excited, I could see that much, and he . . . well, she let him put his arm around her. And I know she never would have done that if she'd been . . . rational. Peggy was as careful as could be.

I walked slowly along with my head down, thinking, and by the time I'd got to the arbor he was gone. And Peggy didn't say anything about him. I said to myself, "My sister is having secrets from me, and it looks as if something serious was doing. And it's not Love—I know that much. He's just taking advantage of her excitement."

After that I got more and more worried about Peggy. She grew very affectionate with Mother—very. She started to hang around and do things for her, and bring flowers, and read to her, and sit and look at her with tears slowly filling her blue eyes and rolling over.

"Aha, Miss Peggy," I said to myself. "You are planning to leave her, that's why you are so devoted. If it were fear that she'd leave you, you'd look scared, and you don't look scared, you look sorry!"

Then she was sometimes more patient with Father. She even went up and kissed him now and then, and Father never encouraged that sort of "foolishness," as he called it. And other times she would almost defy him, as she never used to dare. She'd just set her lips and look stubborn but yet hopeful, as much as to say: "I can stand it—it's not for very long." I was sure of it.

I knew she met young Wallace on the way to school, just casually, and in the garden too sometimes. Father suspected as much too, and one beautiful moonlit night he announced at supper that he should be out all the evening, and not likely to be in until late.

Off slipped Peggy to her room, and though she came back in a minute I went up too presently, and found she had left the gas lit and pulled the burner way out so it would show.

"She's going to meet him, and Father is going to catch them," I said, and slipped down to warn her. But she'd gone already and all I could do was to trot after. I went by the Gales' yard and the alley, and got over the fence softly in the dark. Sure enough there was Ned Wallace holding her hands and begging for something—at least it looked like that. I slipped in at the door on the fence side just as Father bounced in on the other.

"As I supposed!" Father said. "Exactly as I supposed! Making appointments with young men and meeting them alone in the dark, and under the rose altogether, you indelicate young baggage!"

"Not so indelicate as you think, Father," I said calmly, "when her sister is with her. We have to see our friends somewhere, and you don't like them in the house."

Then he turned on me, of course; called me a meddler and a go-between and all manner of things, and then freed his mind to Ned most vigorously.

Ned wasn't a bit afraid of him. He was a big fellow, and I think he liked the excitement.

"I don't wish to make more trouble for your daughters," he said, "or I would give you a man's opinion of you as a domestic tyrant, but for their sakes I'll wish you a good evening."

He vaulted the fence and was off in no time, and we had to take it all the rest of the evening.

Peggy cried dreadfully in my arms that night. She was greatly touched by my saving her, as she called it.

"I don't wonder you feel so badly," I said. "I sometimes think it's enough to make a girl run away from home. Now if Ned only cared that way . . ."

"He does!" Peggy said. "He does!" And she sat right up in bed. "Now, look here, Ben. I didn't mean to tell you, but you've been so brave and stood between me and Father, and you can see now just how impossible it is to bear it any longer. I am going to run away. Ned does love me, and he says a girl has a right to leave a father like that, that he wonders I've stood it as long as I have. He told me to keep it an absolute secret, even from you—but he didn't think you were sympathetic, that's all. He won't care."

"Of course I'm sympathetic," I protested, and I was. I was awfully sorry for Peggy, but I didn't think Ned was the right man for her.

"Didn't you think I cared, Peggy?" I said. "Why, I've been noticing how thin you were, and nervous. I thought sometimes lately you couldn't stand it much longer."

"I'm not *going* to!" said Peggy. "Listen, Ben—hush!" We were whispering, of course. "I'm going away—with Ned—Tuesday night. Next Tuesday night!" This was Thursday.

"Won't Father catch you?" I suggested.

"No, indeed. Ned is too smart for that! We are to go to New York and take a steamer. He's got the tickets, and we'll be gone before Father knows. We're going to Europe! Think of it! And see Venice and Florence and Rome—and Paris! Oh, Ben, I wish you were going too!" (I knew she didn't really love him.)

"Oh, that's great!" I said. "But when do you get married?"

"On the steamer. Ned has a friend who sails on the same boat—a minister, a college friend of his. He's young, but that's no matter. We take the night train from here and go to a hotel in New York, as brother and sister, you know, and then take the steamer in the morning. See? Here's my engagement ring!" She had it on a ribbon around her neck. The ring was genuine, at any rate.

"Aren't you afraid?" I asked.

"No—not much. I was at first and was very careful. But Ned was very nice about it. He said I was quite right to take every precaution, but he was willing to meet all my doubts. He told me all about the minister and showed me his name in the list of 'about to sail,' and he's shown me our tickets."

"Did you ask him about the license?" I inquired.

"License? What license? No, I didn't. What do you mean, Ben?"

"Oh, perhaps it's different on steamers," I answered, "but mostly you have to have a license to be married."

Peggy had read a good many books, too, but although people *read* enough, they never seem to profit by it. I'd read books enough about runaway marriages, and I knew the difference between a real wild, desperate, honest lover and a Designing Wretch. This seemed to me to be the wretch kind, but I knew I mustn't make any mistakes now.

"How about Mother?" I asked.

Then Peggy said how it broke her heart to leave Mother, but Mother didn't need her. That is, she couldn't do her any good as she was, but that he'd said when they came back she'd be a married woman of independent position (Peggy held her head quite high at that), and that she could offer her mother a home to rest in. If I hadn't been so sorry for Peggy—and so fond of her—I should have been pretty angry with her. To be so easy! To believe everything this man said to her—everything—and never use her brains.

"Have you said goodbye to Jimmie Cushman, Peggy?"

She tossed that pretty head a little and set her lips closer. "No, nor do I intend to. He . . . he wouldn't come and see me any more just because Father told him not to. He doesn't care anything for me—nor I for him. I guess he'll see *that* when I'm gone!"

Mr. Cushman was a theological student and very devoted to Peggy. I had thought at one time that she cared more for him than for anyone, and I wasn't wholly sure to the contrary now.

"Do you . . . love Ned Wallace, Peggy?" I asked.

"Of course," she said promptly. "Do you think I'd marry him if I didn't? He's handsome and rich and of a good family, and we have a full understanding. He says I shall have some money settled on me to do as I like with, and have my own way in everything."

Now I knew my sister pretty well, and she never was sordid. If she loved anybody it didn't matter how poor they were.

Her best friend was the poorest girl in school, couldn't dress even as well as we did—and we never had much but made-overs.

Now here was a foe worthy of my steel. To think of having a romance like that going on right in the family! I didn't intend to let it go far, of course, but it was fun to have it started.

I felt just as sure as could be that he was planning a mock marriage, and then he would desert Peggy in a foreign land, maybe, and he might say she had died over there. He might even kill her! But I felt that was letting my imagination go too far. Ned Wallace did not look as if he would ever kill anybody. As I thought of his good-natured, handsome face, I was willing to admit that perhaps after all he did mean to marry her, but even at that I was determined to interfere.

I knew I mustn't tell Mother, of course. She had quite enough to worry her, and as to Father, if he knew, he might even turn dear Peggy out of doors—renounce her—the way they do. He couldn't disinherit her, because he had nothing for her to inherit, but he might say: "You are no longer a child of mine!"

That always puzzled my logical mind. You can't alter a fact by just saying so, surely. Of course if it's a spouse, you can divorce them, and they are no longer a husband or wife of yours, but your child is your child whether you like it or not. I suppose that it is a mere figure of speech. If it could be a fact I shouldn't mind having Father say it to me.

I dare say, if people ever discover this, and read it, they will think I am an Unnatural Daughter—to be so enraged with my own father. He may be a good citizen and all that, but all I know of him is what I see at home, and that is bad— much worse than I have been able to express. He's so . . . hateful, Father is. He seems to like to make you feel uncomfortable. If you do anything you shouldn't, or make a mistake, he never lets you forget it. Peggy was so good as a child, he never could find fault with her much, but now that the boys were around her so he treated her as if she were *bad,* absolutely.

I didn't mind him so much, personally. He rather approved of my efficiency, and I took care not to thwart him—except in necessary things, like that visit to Grandpa's. That was sort of covered up by Mother's illness, and anyhow it was accomplished. It was a sort of triumph, not an error, so he never referred to it much.

But what I could not bear was his treatment of Mother. She got paler and thinner and more silent; she was irritable, too—used to provoke him even—quite unnecessarily—and then say just the wrong thing. And he'd rasp and rasp with that caustic tongue of his. It was just awful.

And now here was my only sister on the verge of a fatal elopement, with only me to stop her, and that without telling. She mustn't go, that's all. If she so much as started, it would get about, and people would say things. They'd be seen on the cars together, of course.

How could I work it? If I could only change her mind so that she'd give it up. I tried this, tried it all sorts of ways, and I was perfectly astonished to see how determined Peggy was. All these years Father had thwarted her and repressed her and forbidden her, and now she had simply focused all her energies on getting away. Nothing I could say altered her determination.

Ned kept in touch with her—throwing notes in at her window at night. I saw that much. The dear girl even showed me some of his letters, and I didn't blame her for liking them. Such compliments! Such tender consideration! Such perfectly beautiful plans for what they'd do in Europe.

I never did such planning in my life, and the time was short, too. I didn't want anybody to know that my sister was so foolish.

In the novels one way they thwart a Villain like Ned is to bring up a Former Victim and that quite convinces the Future Victim, and she casts him off with scorn. But I didn't know any of Ned's former victims, and if I had—well it didn't seem exactly nice, somehow.

Then I thought of appealing to his better nature. Sometimes in the books they do that. But then suppose he really meant to marry her. He was of age, and Peggy was, too, as far as marrying goes—just eighteen. I should think if a young woman knew enough to marry she knew enough to take care of money, and *vice versa,* but that's the way it is. They were both free agents. Besides I wasn't at all sure that Ned had any better nature. No use telling—no use appealing—no victims in sight. And the time they had set for eloping was coming nearer and nearer.

He used to come, very late indeed, prowling along that alley, and get close to the house, and she'd show a very faint light in her window, and he'd throw in his notes. Then she'd slip out and meet him in the arbor down there. I know because I watched. I was so deadly afraid he'd carry her off prematurely.

Finally I devised this plan. Peggy and I don't look alike a bit, but we're about the same size, and our voices are not very different. I began to poison her mind a little, *very* cautiously, about his habits. Of course she knew his reputation, only she wouldn't believe it. I don't think Peggy knew what being "fast" meant. Of course she loved to talk about him, and I would turn the conversation on the possibilities of his having done this and that, in a sort of extenuating way, and quote from stories and poems. She defended him, of course, enjoyed doing it. She said he told her that he had led a wild life, that he had been horribly lonely and that no one had ever understood his real nature until he met her, that now he knew he had never loved before, and so on. It seemed very convincing to her, and if I even hinted that he had done anything very bad she would flush up and be angry—as angry as you can when you mustn't speak louder than a whisper.

But I had read that if people are even a little in love they are jealous, or that you can make them jealous, and I went to work in the most insidious way. Not like that horrid Iago, but more delicately, until I got her to show real feeling and say, "Nonsense! Of course when a man really loves a woman he would never look at another one. If he did, why that would end it." She insisted that Ned never would, now.

Then I determined to make a sacrifice for my sister's sake.

I suggested to her that ours was not the only garden on that lane, or the only summerhouse, that Lou Masters' arbor was as shady as ours, and that I was quite sure I had seen a young woman in it more than once the very nights that Ned came. (I had. I went in and out of it three times, to be accurate.)

Of course I don't know, but I think she said something to him, for she told me that he had laughed at her for being jealous, and vowed that there absolutely were no others—for him.

Then when the time was almost up I found that she'd sent him word to meet her at eleven-thirty. It was a very dark night, fortunately. I went to bed early. She came up and kissed me and tucked me in, said I had been such a comfort to her, and how she hated to leave me, and that she hoped I would get to know Ned by and by and see how good he was. I was very sober. I held her tight and said that even if things went wrong she would always have me to come back to, that if he was just true to her, that was the main thing.

She started downstairs in good season, so as not to creak, and before she had reached the back door I had dropped down the knotted rope I'd hung from my window, with a long coat and slippers on, and a scarf over my head the way she wore it, and flew down to the alley. Ned was coming along very softly, but before he got to our place I called him softly from the Masters' arbor—called him the name I'd heard Peggy use.

"Come in here," I said, "it's safer." It was a safer arbor—ours was very rickety.

He came, of course. It was close to our place, and made no difference to him.

By the time Peggy got down there he had his arms around me, and I was snuggling up to him. It was very disagreeable, and a good deal dangerous, but I had made up my mind to it.

When I saw Peggy standing there, looking petrified and watching us like a hawk, I said quite softly: "Oh, Ned, are you sure? *Sure* that there isn't anybody else? I heard you were attentive—to Maud Beverly." I had. He was keeping right on being attentive to lots of others, and told Peggy that it was a "blind."

"You foolish girl," he said. (I will say this for Ned Wallace, he has a lovely voice—he's a sort of Siren, I guess—a he-Siren.) "I don't care a bit for her. *You* are the only woman in the world that I love."

That was enough for Peggy. She just turned away, as still as a mouse, and was gone. So was I, in another minute. I said I had to, and just ducked and ran. How I *did* run. Poor Peggy was crying too hard to go fast. I was snug in bed before she got upstairs.

She came straight to me. Poor dear, she was feeling terribly.

"Oh, Ben! You were right!" she said. "He's down there with Lou Masters. I *saw* him with my own eyes!"

She was too angry to cry now; the more she thought of it the angrier she got. What he threw into her window that night didn't count; she thought he was fooling her, and the next day she sent back everything he'd ever sent her and refused to see him again.

Of course in time they might have come to an understanding, but other things happened before that.

They didn't elope anyhow.

CHAPTER SEVEN

I drew a long breath after receiving Peggy that night, but I knew well enough it was only a question of time before she would do something just as foolish—maybe worse.

That very night while I hugged her and comforted her I was thinking, thinking hard. After she sobbed herself to sleep I lay there staring at the white places on the ceiling the street lights made, all frescoed with moving leaf shadows, and planning earnestly.

I fell asleep myself before getting anything worth calling an idea, but next day I simply gave my mind to it. Something *had* to be done.

Here was Peggy, likely to have her whole life ruined for lack of pleasant home conditions. Here was Mother. Dear, patient little Mother, who hadn't a fault unless it was lack of judgment. And, yes, she was a little tiresome sometimes, but who could wonder, worn out as she was. Here was Mother being killed by inches—anybody could see that. And here was Father getting more unbearable every day, in his temper, in his habits, in his looks and manners and everything. Anybody could see that too.

And nobody to do anything but me.

If it had been merely a question of putting up with Father, I could have done that readily enough. One poor parent is not unusual. Some children have two. But it was a question of which I preferred to keep, because Mother was giving out completely.

Now between a good mother and a poor father it is not hard to choose; both preference and duty were clear, and I decided promptly.

Before that, when I was younger, I had tried to reform him, as I think I've written before, but I guess I wasn't old enough—or he was too old. Anyway it didn't seem to work; and things just went from bad to worse. Mother's health was thoroughly broken down, and after the long illness she had that summer and the way he behaved to her then, I finally came to a decision. Father must go.

I thought it out clearly over and over. There were the two of them, one dying by inches before my eyes, the other killing her by inches—and nobody doing anything. Of course some of Mother's friends suspected a good deal of it, but I've noticed there are two little conventions which protect a man in a case like this. In the first place, as to the insiders, the wife must never complain of her husband—that is disloyal—as if he were a king and she were a subject. That shuts her up. In the second place, as to the outsiders, you mustn't interfere between a husband and wife—goodness knows why! Personally I think that if people said, "Mrs. Green, you are driving your husband to drink with that tongue of yours," or "Mr. Brown, you are wearing your wife into the grave by your disagreeableness," it might do some good. But most people seem to swear by those conventions, and nobody does anything.

So I drew a long breath and set my teeth hard. Father Must Go! I said it over until I felt like Cato about Carthage.

It would take time and care to accomplish this, but it was not beyond the bounds of possibility—few things are if you really give your mind to them, and there seemed to be no other way to save Mother.

It has taken me a long time to get a fair estimate of Father, and see how hopeless things were. But as I grew older and Mother grew weaker, she told me more. Not to complain of him—she never would do that—but I could see where the problem lay easily enough.

She told me about her girlhood in a quiet Pennsylvania town. They had always been comfortable and happy. She was scarcely older than Peggy when Father first appeared there, full of some invention that was going to revolutionize the coal industry, I think it was. Mother fell desperately in love with him, girl-fashion, and would marry him, though Grandpa was much displeased. Father was something of an inventor and something of a promoter, but never anything that succeeded. He had a thousand plans for making money, and merely managed to spend it. He spent all he earned, which never was much, and what Mother had, which wasn't much either. Grandpa Chesterton helped him a while, but nothing ever came of it, and finally he grew angry and would not let him have any more. He was willing we should all live with him, for Mother and our sakes. But Father acted so that it became impossible.

I can remember the last visit we made there as a family, and I couldn't have been over seven: the loud talking—the old man shaking a stick—Mother crying—it was dreadfully exciting. After that we never went any more, until I did. Every summer Mother used to look so unhappy when the time came around again.

Finally Grandpa got so uneasy about us that he gave Mother our house, settled it on her somehow so that Father couldn't sell it, and tied it up so tight he could not get it away from her. It was lucky for us that we had the good house and garden, but oh what a bone of contention it was. Father was always wanting to mortgage it to carry out some of his schemes, but he couldn't without Mother's signature, and she never would give it to him. All through my childhood I can remember discussions about that house, he always tormenting Mother about it.

"Woman!" he would say in that slow rasping wooden voice of his—wood with nails in it, "a wife cannot hold anything separately from her husband—they two are one. The house belongs to me, in spite of the wearying laws of this unreliable country. When I can take you back to Scotland there will be far less difficulty in the household. Now perform your duty without more words and sign this at once!"

"This" was a mortgage deed which he had prepared in spite of Mother's protests, and which had been a sore topic of discussion for years.

"I can't do it, Angus!" Mother would cry. "You know I can't! It would not be right. My Father gave me the house to keep—to keep for the children—so that we might be sure of a roof over our heads. He made me promise never to sell or mortgage it, never to let you persuade me into it—it was the condition of the gift. And I can't do it—I can't break my word to my father, Angus. Don't try to make me—I'll die first!"

Mother would get awfully nervous and upset over these discussions, and by the time I was old enough to understand what they were arguing about she had grown so weak she couldn't hold out ten minutes—used to break down and cry.

But Father could hold out for hours. I used to sit by that hole in the floor and take it down in shorthand.

"If you have the power to reason," he would say, "which I sometimes doubt, I can make you see the absurdity and the immorality of your position. Listen now—do not sit crying like an ill-behaved child. In the first place a promise is not binding unless it is made with free will and in full understanding of the circumstances. Now you were coerced by a domineering and unreasonable parent—do not interrupt me! And as to understanding the circumstances, you do not understand them yet, after my logical exposition of all these years. It may be you never will, but I think even a woman can follow this.

"Secondly, a promise has no moral weight against an obvious duty. You were already a wife when you made that promise, and the first duty of a wife is to her husband.

"Thirdly, a promise under duress is null and void in law and reason.

"Fourthly, since the duty of a wife is to her husband and your husband needs to raise money on this house, you have no right to resist him.

"Fifthly, the duty of a mother is to her children; your children need many things they have not for lack of the money to be raised on this house and used by me in legitimate business.

"Now, you with your baseless emotionalism and mulish obstinacy—pure brainless instinctive opposition based on no rational premises—are sinning against both husband and child—defrauding your family of its rightful prosperity! Can you deny that? Answer me now!"

Mother wasn't a bit logical. He would make her admit this and that and the other premise, and then prove his points one after the other, relentlessly, in that dry monotonous voice, and Mother would get all worn out. She'd go back on her admissions and deny his conclusions, and return to her original position after she was, logically, completely driven off it.

So Father grew angrier and angrier. It was irritating, the way Mother wouldn't argue; but then it was more irritating the way he could. And she'd cry and he'd say things that fairly scalded. It was awful.

I don't think Mother would have minded his treatment of her so much—she had a regular talent for suffering—if he had been fair to us children, or if he had been more—well, generally decent.

I don't mean that Father was an immoral man—no, indeed. He didn't even drink in the melodramatic way and "come reeling, rolling home"; he sat quietly at home and drank, and got uglier and uglier in his temper. He didn't beat Mother with a club, nor jump on her, but he would make her listen by the hour to those interminable arguments of his until I have heard her sob and shake for half the night afterward, while he snored.

Peggy never seemed to hear, and I never said I did; what was the use? But I kept a record. Even if I couldn't do anything I liked to know what was going on.

Sometimes I heard Mother say, "Hush, Angus! Do hush! The children will hear you."

"And why should they not hear me?" he would demand. "What I say is reasonable and right and it would be well if they could hear it. They might understand better than you do, and small credit to them!"

After a while I began to keep a kind of record of things Father did—in cipher. I learned about substitution codes from *The Gold Bug,* and in some other books, too. Peggy and I used to have one, and Jennie Gale and I had another; they are easy to make.

I found out quite suddenly one day, after writing to Jennie all about one of Father's meannesses to Peggy, that I felt better just for writing it. It seemed almost like doing something. Afterwards when I got maddest I'd go off alone and write it all down—in cipher—and it did me good.

So I kept a blank book just for Father. It said on the cover: "3iist—xoe$." I would never have told what was in it even under torture. That is, I made up my mind not to, but Mother never interfered with our play. She seemed to think we had a right to keep things to ourselves, and though Peggy wanted to know she didn't use torture. Father never saw it. I began this book when I was just twelve, and in two years' time I was astonished myself to see how it mounted up, and how many kinds of meannesses there were.

I've mentioned how Mother loved flowers. She wanted them everywhere—in her hair, on her dress, all around in vases, and especially on the table. Her other passion was for hospitality. If she could have a table full at every meal, and a parlor full in the evening, she would flush and brighten and shine like a rose in her soft gray dress.

She wasn't an orthodox Friend, but always kept largely to their way of living, and she never seemed to tire of doing things to make people comfortable. She was proud of her cooking, too, and no wonder. It was a natural genius with her. To get up a delicious meal and serve it smoothly, with a tableful of flowers and guests—that would have satisfied Mother in heaven, I think. But Father! He would not have a flower on the table—and would prove to you at an hour's length, if you didn't give in sooner, that to have them there was unsuitable and unhygienic and inartistic and in every way deleterious. But he'd smoke his pipe at the table, I noticed, and it always made Mother sick.

When I was little and we were better off and Father hadn't taken this stand, I can remember Mother sometimes, sitting up there across the roses, and just basking in compliments about her cooking from the friends assembled. But we got poorer and poorer, and Father more and more disagreeable, so that we could never have any company, unless it was the minister. He called, of course, and Mother would ask him to stay to tea, and he sometimes did. Father seemed to have a lingering respect for the Dominie, as he called him, so that he wouldn't be rude to him at the table.

But even then Mother was always broken down next day, having been kept awake and crying most of the night to hear father talk about "the Priest and the Woman," with volumes of ancient history of the most unpleasant description pouring slowly and tediously forth. I thought it was simply insulting to Mother, and it was.

Now I had watched all this for nearly ten years, noticing more and more as I grew older, of course. And, at the rate it went on, another year or two would see Mother either mercifully dead or unmercifully driven crazy. It was the ceaseless irritation, the criticism, and caustic comment, the being hindered in everything she wanted to do, and the uncertainty about money. That is worse than plain poverty. Of course, Father brought home something—paid for the coal and so on—but a lot of that was just on credit, and how Mother did hate a debt. He told her that if she wouldn't let him mortgage the house, he would simply do the same thing by getting in debt, and it would be sold over our heads by the sheriff. But I guess his credit wasn't good enough to really do that.

So I focussed all my attention on this most important problem—how to get rid of Father. This was no light matter. I realized that. I should have Mother on my hands then, and Peggy, too, but I knew the difficulty with her wouldn't last long. It was only a question of steering her into reliable matrimony.

With all the ways I had of earning money I didn't feel

worried about Mother. Besides, I had plans for her. As to her missing Father, I couldn't believe she would. Even if she did, I didn't believe that missing him would be half as bad for her health as having him.

Well, the first thing was to establish friendly relations with Father, as far as possible. There never had been any open break between us. I was wise enough for that, and he was no mind-reader. But now I wanted to get . . . *en rapport,* I think that's what they call it.

I studied him as if he were new. Not just his looks—there was nothing new there except some gray in the red of his thick hair—but his character. I must be sure of him, very sure.

It is surprising how much interest there is in anybody once you really give your mind to them. If it had been only myself I should have become almost fond of him, because when you understand just why a person does a thing you don't mind. Study means interest, and interest is pretty close to affection. I mean to remember that if ever I marry a man who turns out to be disagreeable. I mean to marry, of course, but not for *ever* so long. There are things to do first—lots of them.

Father's strong points were Science and Invention, that I knew, of course. Fortunately, I liked them too, and it was not difficult to do a little extra reading, to ask his opinion or advice, to consult him about things I found rather hard to understand. I never saw anybody who didn't enjoy teaching their favorite topic to anybody who is interested in it. And I believe parents have a very particular fondness for seeing their own traits in their children. It seems flattering, somehow.

Meanwhile I learned a lot about mechanical engineering and electricity and things of that sort. My long acquaintance with our nice librarian helped too. He would tell me of special articles in technical magazines, and I'd tell Father, and we got almost chummy. It was fun, in a way, like walking a tightrope or something like that, to see how far I could go, this way or that, and recover myself quickly if I went too far. He was so easily irritated, so tedious in explanation, and so offensively patronizing. But I did it. I succeeded in establishing an *entente cordiale* with Father.

Peggy had been rather cold to him ever since that time about Ned. I didn't blame her a bit. She devoted herself to Mother more, now. I didn't neglect Mother—not at all. It was really a service to her to keep Father in a tolerable humor, and his mind off her, as it were.

Then, following along naturally on Science and Invention, I took up Scotland. This was the main line of attack. I approached slowly and with great care. Scotch History is really very interesting, especially if you've been brought up on Scott's novels and poems and have kept up with the later authors. Father had a bookcase full of them. It had always seemed foolish to me, with as little money as we had, and a whole public library for nothing, but Father's love for books was hereditary, I guess.

I began to knit a cardigan jacket for him (I should have called it a sweater, but that doesn't matter), and used to get him to read to me out of those beloved books of his while I worked. As I've said before, reading aloud was Father's strong point in domesticity. If he couldn't talk he liked to read—interminably.

Well, I plowed and harrowed and seeded the soil. I became a better authority on Scotland than he was himself, almost. I knew all those old kings and chieftains, way back to the Roman invasion, and the legends and ballads—thousands of them. One thing I found that pleased me—that most of those nice ballads and songs were written by women, but I never dwelt on that. Where there was a doubt, Father always denied it; and when it was an established fact, he ignored it.

Our own line was the background of it all. I got him to make a genealogical tree, working out all he knew of our kith and kin, and it joined with a great many printed ones that covered the kings of ancient Europe, and went back to Noah's Ark.

Father and I had a very pleasant time; he almost complimented me once in a while. But his business worried him, and since Mother remained so feeble that even he hardly dared to harry her now, he got to confiding his troubles to me—or parts of them. That he was homesick for Scotland I knew; that fire I kept burning all the time. It was not only our talk and reading, but I got Peggy to play Scotch airs to us evenings. And when she said she hated everything Scotch and never wanted to hear any of their screeching music any more, I just had a good talk with her. I told her if she would play and sing Scotch things for me for another few weeks I wouldn't ask her to again for . . . three years. I'd have said "ever," but you never know for sure that you may not want a thing again. It is well to be economical, even with promises. So she used to sit down after supper (Mother always went to bed early now, the doctor said she must) and just drift along with old Scotch melodies, and sing now and then, and I'd lay my book down and ask Father things about Scotland until he'd get up and walk the floor, let his pipe go out, and even forget his tumbler of toddy while he talked of his native land. He got more homesick than ever.

Then I gradually found out that one reason he wanted to get over there was that he was convinced there was coal on his land and that if he were only on the spot he could make sure. The work he did here might stop any day, he said gloomily. He used to get more confidential toward the end of the evening, when Peggy had gone to bed, too, and I sat knitting. It was then I gathered finally that he was more or less in debt— on his own account, I mean, not just the house.

"You have a fairly good head, for a girl, Benigna," he said to me. "Can ye not see that if only that poor mother of yours would let me raise a bit of money on this house of hers we could all win out clear?"

"What is she afraid of?" I asked. "That we should lose the house?"

" 'Tis just woman's foolishness!" He got up and walked about, swinging his long arms. "She cannot sell it, and I do not ask her to, but she could mortgage it—for a little. That I could pay off in a year or two at most, and no risk at all."

"I've heard you speak of a deed—is that what you mean?" I asked cautiously. "That doesn't sound very terrible."

"It is not terrible, it is plain common sense. But your

mother won't see it. You cannot argue with a woman." And he sat down disgustedly.

"Perhaps when she's a little better she'll feel differently. Could you explain about that deed to me, Father? Maybe if I understood it I could persuade Mother a little."

He showed it to me without any difficulty—had it in his pocket. It was all made out solemn and legal as could be, everything ready but Mother's name to be signed.

" 'Tis only a miserable thousand dollars that it calls for," he said, as if a thousand dollars was no more than a pittance. "Then I could clear off these trifling matters that annoy me here, and have enough left to make the voyage—and what little it would take over there. There's nothing in the way but your mother's obstinacy!" And he'd march again, and talk about "these women."

"If you were there, Father, could you live on your estate?" I asked with a serious face.

"Live on it! We could all live on it!" he protested. "There's a house and a garden and a sheep run—do I not draw an income from it, as you know?"

He did, and I did know. I'd been figuring on it very carefully. If there were any way on earth of getting him over there I thought the place would keep him in decent comfort.

Then I made a little arrangement through an old school friend of mine, Mary Howard, who had gone to England to live with her father's people. We used to correspond in cipher. I was very fond of Mary. She was trustworthy, and thought a good deal of my judgment; I had helped her out of a scrape once or twice.

I sent her a typewritten message in an addressed envelope, and asked her to send it to the *Edinburgh Weekly News and Observer*. That was the paper Alison took. She would have a paper of her own, wouldn't be contented with a secondhand one, but was proud to let Father read it, and he said there was no reason why we should take two. There was a postal note to pay for the advertisement; I had that much in my Secret Hoard. Grandpa had given me a generous allowance to come home with, too, and I always had a little something.

I told Mary to please change the note into stamps at a post office not near to her home, and put them into the envelope. "Please insert the enclosed advertisement for the issue of October 3rd. Stamps for payment enclosed." That was the message. And keep it a Dead Secret, for my sake, I told her. I said she was welcome to read it, but perhaps she'd be safer if she knew nothing whatever about it.

Mary was a cautious person. She walked a mile and a half to change that note, and never peeked into the envelope at all—just sealed and sent it, after tucking in the stamps. She wrote me all about it.

I kept close watch for that paper to come, which it did in time. Alison read it solemnly through in the afternoon, sitting in her painfully clean kitchen by the window. She got her work done like a sort of cold whirlwind, and then used to sit there with a big, stiff white apron on, and not a sound but the flies on the sticky paper. I borrowed the *News and Observer* just before she went to bed and, yes, there it was.

So I put the paper down on the little stand by Father's elbow and sat down by the lamp with my knitting. Peggy had been playing for an hour or so; the room still seemed to be crooning with "The Land o' the Leal" and "Auld Lang Syne." Nobody was up now but just us. He read along, and read along. I thought he'd never come to it. But by and by he gave a start and sat there staring.

"What is it, Father?" I said, and half rose to my feet, but he folded the paper up tight, and put it in his pocket. I knew what he had read, well enough:

If the next of kin to the late Andrew Angus MacAvelly of this city will call in person within 10 days at 109 Blackie St., Edinburgh, it will be to the advantage of the family.

I had been at great pains with the working of that advertisement. 109 Blackie Street was the address of a firm of engineers. I thought they could advise him about that coal—maybe. As to the advantage of the family, I was sure of that.

He was pacing up and down now, very grim indeed.

"Father," I said, "you don't look well. I wish you could

get a vacation somehow. I believe if you were better Mother would be, too."

He stopped short and stared at me. "Benigna," he said grimly, "by a singular coincidence I was making up my mind to take a trip at once. It is only a question of persuading your mother. . ."

I didn't like the way he said "persuading."

"See here, Father," I said, "I know you could in time, but I wish you'd let me try. You know sometimes she'll listen to me, and it will save you the worry. Just let me take the deed. If I can get it signed without her realizing that you're going, I think that will be easiest. She's so weak now, you know."

He showed me the paper presently; he just had to talk to somebody.

"Here it is, maybe the chance of a lifetime. I must go, and go at once. It'll be the making of our fortunes."

"I tell you, Father, let me pack your things, and you start off right away without getting Mother excited. Isn't this Thursday? Isn't there a boat going Saturday usually? Could you get the money tomorrow, if you had that deed? And go off tomorrow night, and then write Mother a letter from New York before sailing?"

We began to plan. He was as excited as a boy.

"If you can do that, Ben, you can do me a service. Just get her to sign it, if you can. I have a man ready and waiting with the money." (Part of it was owing him. That was why he was so willing, I found out later.)

"Will it be enough, Father?" I asked anxiously.

"It will be enough to get me there, at any rate, I can manage afterward. There will be more when I get to work over there."

It was late before we went to bed. There was so much to talk over. But I assured him that I could get the signature early in the morning, and that his best plan was not to disturb her at all.

"I'll tell her you were called away on business," I said. "And Peggy and I'll take good care of her. We can get along for a month or so all right—or until we hear from you."

I packed his bags for him—he said he didn't need a trunk—and that he could buy things on the other side far better and far cheaper. He looked quite eager and young—fairly smelled the heather already. He planned for a very early start, but he was up so late that he didn't wake at all in the morning until I slipped in, with the deed in my hand, all signed and acknowledged.

"She's asleep again," I said, "and Peggy's not awake. They'll understand that you had to go in a hurry."

He looked at the document carefully before he hurried off. "How ever did you persuade her?" he demanded.

But I just reached up and kissed him goodbye. "Hurry up!" I said. "So long as she's not worried it doesn't matter, does it? Be sure and bring me some cairngorms when you come back, won't you?"

So off he went in a sort of clumsy rush, and I watched him go, "a prey to conflicting emotions." Everything was as still as could be in the house, and nothing moving in sight but a milk wagon. I felt like Lady Macbeth, or—who was that girl in the turban who killed her father?—or they said she did.

Then I drew a long breath.

"Now, Benigna Machiavelli," I said to myself, "you've got to take care of your mother and sister. And it's no crime to sign your own name, that I know of!"

CHAPTER EIGHT

You needn't imagine that I let Father go off without having some sort of provision in mind for Mother. I had been studying Mother all my life, more or less, and had a theory as to what would make her happiest.

It's particularly hard to understand your own parents. They stand so close to you and they are always there. It's like living on the side of a mountain—you can't see it.

Of course you love them, at first anyway, and admire them, and all that. Then, if they turn out to be conspicuously unpleasant, like Father, you have to struggle with your upbringing to recognize it.

Of course I know the commandment "Honor thy father and mother," as a means to longevity. But if your father drinks, and isn't any earthly use, and abuses your mother, can you honor that? I couldn't, and I'm willing to die sooner, if that's the consequence.

Then again, once you begin to criticize and blame a parent it is hard to do them justice—they are so near. The child—the little thing that has looked up to the big thing for so long—all his or her life—cannot easily see around a parent's faults when she or he first recognizes them, cannot make allowances and be patient. If I'd been thirty or forty I might have been more patient with Father, maybe, but I would have assisted his departure just the same. It was the best thing possible under the circumstances.

The great difficulty with Mother was her patient discouragement. I couldn't seem to get her ambitious for anything.

"My life is over," she used to say patiently. "I must not complain. You girls have your lives before you. You will go on and marry and be happy, I hope, and I will live in your happiness. A mother's life is in her children."

Now I loved Mother enough, I'm sure of that. But I wasn't at all contented with this prospect of her just living around in Peggy's and my happiness all the rest of her life. If it was just metaphorical, that would be a very slim sort of diet for her. And if meant practically, to live in our houses after we were married, that didn't seem to be fair to any of us. I've seen it done, lots of times.

When one gets to be a genuine, well-established Grandma —cap and glasses and soft shoes—it's all right; there's no other right place for a real helpless, amiable Grandma. But for an able-bodied, middle-aged woman to try to be a professional Grandma at forty or fifty, it doesn't fully employ her faculties.

Here was my dear mother, only forty years old—young, for a man, and by no means aged for a woman. Living in a daughter's happiness—even two daughters' happiness—is not a sufficient occupation for a middle-aged woman. Sometimes, being still active and having no other field of interest, they mess up the daughter's happiness a good deal. I've seen that done too.

So I used to sit and look at dear Mother with those noncommittal eyes of mine. (I was always proud of my eyes. They were so inexpressive; they didn't give me away.) And I'd wonder how I could get her roused up to see that she ought to have ten, twenty, thirty years of satisfying life before her, with lots of happiness of her own, to use and give away. She thought it was all over with her life on account of Father, but what sort of a life did she have with him?

I had a secret conviction that there was a stretch before her which she would find much pleasanter than what lay behind. So I had planned out a career for Mother.

Our assets were the house, and Mother's motherliness. Of course, the obvious thing was boarders. I'd had that in mind for some years, more or less, and had been studying the business, as far as I could.

There was Mrs. Gale next door. She kept boarders because she had a house, and a daughter to bring up, and no other business. But she didn't like it, and Jennie didn't like it, and the boarders didn't like it. Mrs. Gale was an awfully cross woman. Jennie said it was nervous trouble, that naturally she was lovely, but I guess I never saw her when she was natural. Nervous or not, the servants couldn't stand it. They wouldn't ever stay long. Mrs. Gale worked and fussed and scolded, but somehow the house was never clean, in spite of always being cleaned. That is, things were continually torn up, and there was dust and flapping, but none of that still freshness that feels so good in a room.

She wanted Jennie to do more work in the house, but Jennie hated housework, and wanted to be a stenographer and typist. She said she could earn enough to take care of her mother that way, and would much rather.

I backed her up, told her what wages expert stenographers got, and how keeping boarders wasn't a bit good for her mother, and it was really her duty to struggle on even if scolded—for her mother's sake. So she struggled.

I taught her stenography. It was good for both of us. We took turns dictating, and I tried to keep her spirits up. But what with keeping on at school, and helping her mother, and our night work besides, it was very hard on Jennie. If it hadn't been for me she would have given it up, I know. But I used to figure out for her what fine pay she would get by and by, and how she and her mother could have a little apartment and live so comfortably on that, how it was really for her mother's good, and she must bear up for her sake. So Jennie hung on.

Mrs. Gale's house was close to her side of the fence, and ours was close to our side. They were both big, comfortable, elderly houses, with plenty of rooms, and built on about the same plan by a rich family who lived there once—brothers or sisters or something. They used to have a covered way connecting them, but that had been taken away later, when the estate changed hands.

Grandpa Chesterton, I think, may have had a sort of half thought of the professional advantages of the place when he bought our house, but if he hadn't, I had now. You see it was only ten minutes' walk from the city hall, but owing to the sudden hill it was quiet and pleasant—a nice residential street, yet close to business.

With such a house and such a mother, boarders were the obvious resource, but there was Mrs. Gale. She had rather prejudiced Mother.

"Oh, Mrs. MacAvelly," she would say, sitting rocking in our parlor when she ought to have been attending to business, "don't let anything ever induce you to take boarders. Such a care! And such an expense! And so ungrateful! And the trouble one has with servants. It is bad enough in a private family, but in a boarding house!"

She would rock and fan herself and complain, telling how three of her young gentlemen had failed to pay their bills last year, and how one had left a trunk, which turned out to have nothing in it but worn-out clothes and newspapers and coal. "My own coal, too, Mrs. MacAvelly!"

And Mother would agree with her sweetly, and accept all her misadventures as a needful part of the business, and thank her stars that she didn't have to keep boarders.

I was pretty good friends with Mrs. Gale. Saturdays she would sometimes take me to market with her. I'd offer to carry the basket, and she would complain to me, just as she did to

Mother, of the direful disadvantages of her business.

"Why do you do it, Mrs. Gale?" I asked her.

"To keep a home for Jennie, of course," was her reply. "A mother must do many things for a child whether she likes it or not."

"How would you prefer to live if you could?" I inquired.

"When Jennie has a position as teacher," she said, "then we shall board."

She said it with a good deal of determination, an expression of great relief. Also, I thought, she had a vengeful glitter in the eye, as if she, in boarding, would wreak on some future landlady all the injury she had suffered from her own boarders.

Meanwhile I studied her methods of marketing—and learned how not to do it.

Well, I had all this in my mind, and put out some feelers, as it were, before Father left.

I kept his going from Mother quite successfully. If she had known, I'm sure she'd have tried to keep him. Mother never did know when she was well off. If she thought it was her duty to have a fox gnawing at her vitals she would have absolutely petted that fox. I respect duty as much as anyone, but I do think there is room for some discrimination.

As to telling her about that mortgage, all at once, right there on the garden path, with Father in a disappearing street-car, the idea struck me that perhaps she needn't know, after all. The man who was to lend the money on it lived in New York now—old Mr. Burt. I'd seen him. He would never bother us if his interest was paid—eight percent, it said in the deed, $80.00 a year. That wasn't so much—about $1.50 a week—surely I could earn more than that! I sat down on the steps and figured it out, then and there. Anyway she need not know until she was better.

But that meant a new crime—intercepting letters. I felt sure I could catch the first one, but Father would write

more of course. I couldn't be certain of getting them all.
Then I thought of that old rhyme:

> Oh what a tangled web we weave,
> When first we practise to deceive.

But it didn't trouble me any. I love tangled webs; it's such fun
to tangle and untangle them.

Then I thought of a fine thing, and I was mortified that
I hadn't thought of it before, but it had taken all my intellect
to manage Father.

I determined to stop that first letter, just tell Mother that
Father had gone to Scotland. I'd not tell her how he got the
money, except that he borrowed it, and not that, unless she
asked. Meanwhile I'd get Grandpa to take her away for a visit.
I had other plans to get started before she came back.

So I wrote a nice letter to Grandpa, told him that now
Father had gone abroad I thought Mother would be willing
to take a trip somewhere for her health. He'd asked her to
before, but she never would leave Father. I told him how really
miserable she was, and that the doctor said she must have
change of air and scene, and that we girls could get along
perfectly with Alison.

When I took up Mother's breakfast and she had had her
coffee and was leaning back on the piled-up pillows looking
like a faded pink sweet pea, I told her in a casual, offhand
way that Father had gone off on a business trip and left her
in my care. She looked anxious at once.

"Where's he gone, Ben?" she said. "When did he go?
When's he coming back?" And then she shut her eyes, and little streaks of tears ran down. "He didn't even say goodbye to
me," she said, very softly. Mother was as weak as that.

"Now Motherkins, you mustn't mind," I said. "It's a
business trip. I didn't want to worry you about it and really
I persuaded him to go off without telling you. He'll write
presently, dear. Meanwhile you must get as well as you can
so as to astonish him when he comes back. Please forgive me,
Mother, if I did wrong."

Mother would forgive anybody for the asking, especially us children, and she didn't ask any more questions, except, "Did he say how long he'd be gone?"

"No, he didn't, but then it must be quite a good while."

I thought rapidly and decided that she ought to know as much as possible about it, so as to be settled in her mind. So I told her frankly that he had seen an advertisement in the Edinburgh paper and had started for Scotland.

She looked at me with her large eyes. "How could he, Benigna! Where'd he get the money?"

"He was going to borrow it, Mother, of a man in New York. He took an early train on purpose. I think he thought you might disapprove. Anyway I'm the one to blame, so if you've forgiven me, you'll have to forgive him. And really I think it will do Father lots of good. He has seemed actually homesick lately. Just seeing his native land again will make him happy."

Peggy was tremendously interested when she heard of it, and Alison McNab was not only interested but angry.

"He has gone to Scotland, is it, and not a word to me? I should have been glad to send messages to my people there, and presents perhaps. Gone to Scotland—without a word!"

Peggy sat with Mother, and Alison of course was busy enough, but my main occupation now was to watch for the postman. I could see him coming up James Street, if I kept a steady eye on one place between the trees, and then it was easy to meet him between the corner and our house.

"Good morning, Mr. Reilly. Any letters for us?"

There weren't any at all, so I had it all to do over for the noon mail. But Father had forgotten, or been in too much of a hurry maybe, and only sent a hasty word on steamer paper just before starting. It came next day.

I smuggled it up to my room, steamed it, opened it, and read it, feeling more Machiavellian than ever in my life. To my great satisfaction it didn't say a word about the deed and the money. I suppose he couldn't bear to thank her. So Mother got her letter all right, and felt relieved in her mind.

Then I put my trust in Providence. "Perhaps he'll never mention it," I thought to myself.

Meanwhile Grandpa had come. He didn't write, he didn't even telegraph. He just came.

"Pack up her things, Benigna!" he said. "She's going back with me. She can have 'rest and change' there for a while, and then we'll see."

He wanted me to come too, but I urged that Peggy ought to be the one this time.

"Peggy's so sweet with Mother," I told him. "I'll be all right here with Alison. There's a lot of housecleaning and things to do."

"You must have some money to live on, child," he said, and left me enough for some time. Grandpa would have been glad to support us all—without Father. But Mother had that stubborn sense of loyalty. She would not do what Father disapproved, no matter how unreasonable he was.

Grandpa's coming in that way made my work almost too easy, but I guess I needed some leeway, after all, for I was undertaking a good deal.

"May I do what I think necessary in the house, Mother?" I asked before they went.

"Yes indeed, child. Whatever you want to do will be wise, I'm sure," she said. Mother had a high idea of my judgment— even from what little she knew of it.

"Now I *am* a housekeeper, Grandfather," I boasted with pride. "You'll trust me to manage right, won't you?"

"I'll back you as a housekeeper against all comers, Benigna. But you ought to have some older person with you."

"I'm going to get Miss Ayres to come, if she will," I said. "Or maybe Miss Arthur—some of the teachers. I shall have quite a boardinghouse to manage. May I run a boardinghouse, Mamma?"

"It'll be all right if Miss Ayres will come—do get her," she said.

And Grandpa said, "Go ahead with your boardinghouse, child. You're equal to it."

Peggy heard them, and Alison, who was putting in Mother's bags and fussing around generally. So I had quite a cloud of witnesses. Of course they didn't think I would, but what of that?

The carriage drove off, Mother quite rosy and hopeful-looking, Peggy as pretty as a whole bunch of fresh roses, and Grandpa happy enough to get his daughter back for a time.

Alison stood there for a while, her arms folded, watching them go. "'Tis a good thing," she said. "A mighty good thing! It will make a well woman of her, belike." Then she went back to her kitchen and I stood there by the gate alone.

Never in my life had I felt such a sense of hope and power. To have Father gone was like . . . well, did you ever hear one of those big city coal wagons unloading down an iron chute? It takes ever so long and all the neighborhood is scraped by that dull rasping roar. If you're busy you don't notice it, much, but when the thing *stops*, such a soft, cool, rested feeling comes over you—

> And silence like a poultice came
> To heal the wounds of sound.

Having Father gone was like that.

Having Mother gone was not a pleasure in that way, of course, but it was a relief of another sort not to have to worry about her. Nothing could be better for her, I was sure, than Grandpa's big, shady house, and that lovely place of his with the certified milk and eggs, and the flowers.

Having Peggy gone was a loss—I did miss Peggy always. But then she too had been a care lately. Now she was off my hands for a while. There weren't any young men at Grandpa's farm, except the workmen, and when I remembered that man on the train struggling so when Grandpa collared him I didn't worry about Peggy.

So there I was, eighteen years old, healthy and strong, quite a sum of money in my pocket, and A House, to do as I liked with. And it was only the last week in April.

I stood very tall and lifted my chest. I felt as if I was a Giant, a Giant let out from under something. Or the Jinni out of the Jar.

The first thing I did was to take Alison into my confidence. Into some of it, I mean. She was not so much a servant as a Retainer, a real friend of the family. Though not given to praising anybody, I knew she had a good opinion of me in some ways.

I waited a few days and took a favorable time—afternoon, the work all done and she pretty well rested anyway, there was so little to do now.

"Alison," I said seriously, "how would you like to earn some extra money this summer?"

She looked at me suspiciously, but merely replied, "I'd like it fine."

"Here's a big house with a lot of empty bedrooms, all comfortably furnished, and two big parlors besides the library and dining room. Here's a garden big enough to raise a lot of small vegetables, besides our berries and fruit. And here is a woman of exceptional ability and skill," I bowed to her, "and a young woman who can make herself useful."

She nodded noncommittally. "Aye," she said.

"You know Mother wants me to get Miss Ayres or somebody to stay here while she's away, and you heard her say—and Grandpa, too—that I might have a 'houseful of boarders' if I liked. Well now, I'm thinking of getting a few real nice people that Mother knows, friends of hers, to come and board here, for the summer anyway. I won't charge them much, but if I can raise most of the vegetables it won't cost much to feed them. And I was thinking of offering you half a dollar a week extra, for each of them. I can do all the bedroom work and wait on table.

"Then if you felt strong enough you could do some of their washing and make that much more. And besides that, if you can make real economical dishes—they've got to be fed well and plenty of it but it doesn't need to be expensive—if you can make the cost come under what I've allowed for food, you shall have the difference."

Alison's little eyes sparkled. It was fun to watch her. The Scotchness of her came out so strong. Canny was no word for it. She asked no end of questions: Who was I going to get? How did I know they would come? How could I be sure they would pay their bills? And so on.

I told her they would have to pay in advance and that Dr. Bronson and Mr. Cutter were going to back me up. I had asked them.

She agreed after a while

"The difficult point is the feeding," I told her earnestly. "We've got to feed them well—very well—and have it look profuse. Yet at the same time we must have all we can—your extra profit comes in there. But if you skimp them they'll not stay."

She looked annoyed. "Do I not know that, child? Would I kill the goose that lays the golden eggs! Let me advise with you about the marketing, and do you fill your garden with the small things that count up so fast. Who's going to do the work in that garden, by the way?"

"I am, of course."

"You'll be busy, I'm thinking."

"I like to be busy." Alison hadn't any idea of how strong I was, nor how ambitious. How should she have?

"It's only women you're planning for?" she asked suddenly. "If you have men they want a big joint fresh every day, but women like little made dishes."

"Only women so far," I said.

So we started in.

First I engaged a man to plow and harrow, and I planted ever so many things. I spent a lot of time working in that garden besides what I spent in reading up about it. It looked like a Chinese one before long, so neat and thoroughly filled, and as soon as one thing was out, in went something else. We had young radishes and lettuce and peas all summer long.

We began with Miss Ayres. She came within a week, and she thought her two sisters might come if they liked it. I told her to ask them to visit us for a week, and see.

Mr. Cutter was very much interested in my plan. I told him it was good practise for me, would keep Alison busy, and that I hoped to have a nice little sum for Mother when she got back. He sent us two nice women from his church, friends of Mother's.

But Dr. Bronson was the best. He was Mrs. Gale's star boarder and had two rooms on the ground floor. He looked me up and down with those twinkling little eyes of his.

"You're a young schemer, Benigna," he said. "But I think this is a good scheme. You want to surprise your mother with a fat little nest egg, do you? Well, you must have people who stay in town all summer. With Miss Ayres for a chaperon you might have a man or two."

I told him what Alison said about hot joints.

"One that I have in mind is a vegetarian," he said. "And the other is a patient of mine on a diet—I prescribe the diet, my dear. He's fussy, but will pay anything for what he wants. Then I've another patient or two. How many do you want?"

I told him I thought we might accommodate ten, but that one thing was absolutely necessary: they must be the kind of people Mother would like.

"What's that to do with this summer?" he asked.

Then I looked as ingenuous as one of Wordsworth's cottage maidens. I said that if anything should delay Father's return I thought it might be possible that Mother would like to keep on with some of them, that perhaps it would interest her and keep her from worrying.

"You know she likes company," I told him.

He nodded sagaciously. "You've a good head, child. I've always said so." And then he fell to thinking.

The house was as fresh as paint and everything was clean.

Alison wore the air of a mighty general. Miss Ayres sat at the head of the table. She was as interested as could be. What Grandpa left me was enough for all I had done, and some extra linen and table things.

By the middle of May we began with eight people, averaging $10.00 a week—that's $80.00.

No rent, no extra fires, being summer; no extra service—except the $4.00 to Alison, and the $1.00 a week for a woman to help her on washing day. I allowed $2.50 a week apiece for their food. And, if you'll believe me, Alison saved off that. You see our garden gave us a lot of green vegetables and fruit, and we had the preserves and pickles already made to fall back on. Alison's soups were a wonder, and they cost practically nothing—just the bones we had left over—and we had our onions and carrots and parsley. Then she made "rechaufées" that melted on the tongue, and her tricks with rice and potatoes were beyond praise.

We used to plan menus a week ahead, dovetailing in. It was a wonder how good things were, and another wonder how little they cost. That culinary magician actually cleaned up another half-dollar a week apiece of herself, and she earned it. It takes brains and hard work to make a liberal, attractive, varied bill of fare of inexpensive materials.

There are some things that everybody likes. Cleanliness and quiet and no flies, for instance. Nice china and table linen. Long sheets, light blankets in summer—not those uncomfortable "comfortables"—and light bedspreads too, for hot weather. Plenty of towels, and good-sized ones. And wastebaskets.

Fortunately we had two bathrooms, and I was in and out of them all day keeping them clean. I had some of those small hand towels in there too.

The food business has necessities: one is enough to eat, real substantial good food. Whatever else was on the table I always saw to it that there was at least one copious dish—rice or potatoes or gingerbread—but lots of it, so as to make them feel they could eat freely. And good quality of course. The next thing is looks—most everybody likes to have their food look nice. I made quite a specialty of table decoration. The third is variety. Now there's fruit. I used to have a great piled-up dish for breakfast, many kinds. Perhaps bananas and apples most, but five or six kinds. It looked lavish, but didn't cost any more than the same amount of one. And I made long lists of odd things out of books and magazines, and saw to it that there was something new almost every day.

They talked about our table all over town, those boarders did, and I don't suppose one of them ever figured out the relative cost of those delicacies. Hash is a horror, but croquettes and ramekins and hot stuff in scallop shells, that's different.

I allowed myself $5.00 a week for my work—and I earned it!

I worked an hour before breakfast in the garden, waited on eight people, had eight beds to attend to, and the downstairs work. I was always busy enough to suit my ambitions.

And there was $40.00 a week over, clear splendid profit, to astonish Mother with and show her what she could do.

I wrote Mother about it, little by little; that Miss Ayres had come, that she had brought sisters, that Dr. Bronson had asked me to try a patient of his, a dear soul who needed careful diet. I wrote that he'd sent another patient who was a vegetarian, and then one more. I dare say Mother thought they were women, but I didn't say so, I said "patients."

It was easier because Grandpa decided to take Peggy and her on an ocean trip—not to Scotland, mind you. He just bought the tickets and haled them away at a day's notice, as it were. I wondered if Peggy had had any desperate admirers to start him off like that.

Anyway they went, and when Mother came back about the end of September she looked like a different woman.

CHAPTER NINE

The money part of keeping boarders is easy. You have to find out how many, and at what rate, will pay enough more than their food costs to enable you to provide room, labor, and a profit. Having established that, you then have only to make it so attractive to this number of people that they will come, and stay. That's all very simple.

I found out before the summer was half over that there are always people wanting to be taken care of, people who only board where they do because they know of no better place.

My carefully selected few had friends and acquaintances, of course. They all talked about our table, and invited their friends to meals—75^{c} for dinner, 50^{c} for lunch, 25^{c} for breakfast—and presently we had a waiting list.

No, the difficulty about boarders is not getting them in, it's getting them out!

I made one mistake, and had so much trouble on account of it that it has taught me the lesson of a lifetime. Fortunately Mother was not at home, or I should never have been able to set it right. She is so yielding.

This was another patient of Dr. Bronson's, a rich, middle-aged, invalidish sort of person, willing to pay anything for what she wanted, he said. A Mrs. Miller—Mrs. Joseph Rawlings Miller, she insisted on, though Mr. Miller was dead, and Mr. Rawlings even more so, if possible. She'd had two of them.

She was so anxious to come, and willing to pay so much that I agreed to let her have one of the parlors downstairs. She said she would bring her own bed, she preferred to. If that had been all!

She brought a whole load of furniture, heavy overpowering sort of things, and a parrot! Dr. Bronson never said she had a parrot, and when I went with him to see her it was not in sight. She had been very gentle and polite when I called. I didn't *like* her, but she offered to pay $15.00 a week, and I rapidly counted up how much extra that would be, and . . . well, I admit I was a fool—once.

It was not the furniture that made the trouble, nor the parrot, though that was bad enough. She turned out to be one of those people who have a natural gift for setting other people by their ears.

First she'd made violent friends with one of my nice boarders, and then with another. She'd invite them to matinees, make them presents, take them to ride—all sorts of attractions. And then, extracting as many confidences as she could from each one, she'd make use of her information with the others.

The way I knew this was because she tried it first on me. She thought I was so young and, well, ordinary, that I should be easy. Little did she imagine how I spelled my name—secretly.

It gave me quite a shock, really, when she began. It was the first time I had met an actively designing person, except for Grandpa's housekeeper, and her designs were very limited.

But to have this large, beaming, cordial lady begin to ask delicate questions about my father and mother, and Peggy, and our circumstances generally, I had to put on all my armor at once. Even with my two handicaps, not telling lies and always keeping up my innocent, ingenuous aspect, I think I did pretty well.

Once she asked something about Father, and for the life of me I could not think of any way to get around it. So I just looked as girlish as I could and said that I didn't think Mother'd be willing for me to talk about my father—even to her. This with a bright smile.

She liked the place, though I learned afterwards how she had criticized it to some of the others. But she made more trouble than any six of them, always wanting things just a little different, hotter, or colder, or something. Worst of all she would bustle out into the kitchen, absolutely giving orders to Alison. It was enough to break up our entire household.

The money she paid wasn't a circumstance. Two of my nice teachers, who had been bosom friends, quarrelled before two weeks were over, and left—both of them.

I filled the rooms, but there was a week between. And I saw more trouble brewing, a sort of coolness between Miss Ayres and her sister, a young music teacher getting tremendously affectionate with Mrs. Miller, and then beginning to make eyes at the Vegetarian Man, who didn't like it.

"This'll never do," I said to myself. "She's got to go, and quickly." And I began to plan in earnest.

The Gales had a big brindled yellow tomcat,"Jerusalem, the Golden," they called him, a real fierce one; dogs were afraid of him. That is, dogs who had made his acquaintance. He was a great friend of mine, Jerry was, and was used to the house. It was desperately careless of me to leave Mrs. Miller's door open when she was out, and the front door too, and then go away upstairs. I apologized most amply, but what good did that do. She never knew whether someone stole the bird, or if he flew away of his own free will. There was a feather or two about, I believe, but she couldn't prove anything by that.

Well, that was only the parrot, but it was some gain. I hope whoever caught him was nicer than she was. She used to tease the poor bird to distraction, and then be desperately affectionate.

Then I considered deeply, with this result: we were sitting in the front parlor one evening after dinner, and I asked if they had ever heard such and such a story—something I had read about—about premonitions and things. They were interested right off. Everybody always seems possessed to play with that subject—anything occult. Then one of them told of a telepathic communication her mother had had, and another boasted an aunt who was clairvoyant. I asked a few questions, and drew out the more quiet ones—everybody had something. Mrs. Miller, of course, had plenty to say. Her experiences were more surprising than any, and more thrilling.

Then all at once I asked to see her hand, walked across the room and looked at it carefully, without saying a word. Only I grew very quiet all at once.

"What do you see, child?" she demanded.

"I'd rather not commit myself," I said, with a little laugh. "I don't really understand palmistry much." I didn't, that was a fact. But I went on looking at some of the others, and then went back, asking to see her other hand, and shaking my head over that, too. She got quite excited, and insisted that I should tell her what I saw, or thought I saw.

"Why, it's nothing," I said. "I oughtn't to speak of it at all. I'm not an expert. And it might just frighten you—only you wouldn't be so foolish as to be frightened over such nonsense, would you?"

She protested that she wouldn't, and that I really must tell her.

"There's nothing to tell," I said, as if I was ashamed of my limitations. "It's only, well, I don't see your life going on . . . after a certain point." They were all feeling sort of creepy by this time, with all the talk we'd had, and I said it with just that little deprecatory, suggestive air.

She turned a little pale, and then I was sure she panted a little, but she wanted to know which point. Of course any point would do—I'm no forecaster of people's lives. I just said, "Oh, I tell you what we'll do. Let's have Alison come in. Alison is Scotch—she has second sight. Perhaps she can tell us something, really."

So after a good deal of persuading Alison came in, looking very clean and starchy in her big, white apron.

She said it was "a' nonsense!" But I wheedled her. Most

of my wheedling had been done before. I had quite thrown myself on her mercy and begged her to help me out, lest our flourishing little business be ruined. She didn't want to lose what she was making, and she knew as well as I that it would be a lovely thing for Mother, so she let herself be persuaded. And once she began, she did spendidly. I wouldn't have believed she had it in her.

First she sat quite still, with fixed staring eyes. Then she began to rock gently back and forth, and make a queer low crooning sound. It got on our nerves awfully, even mine.

Then she got up stiffly and walked to first one and then the other of us, looking for all the world like a sleepwalker. Over some she would nod, or smile a little, at others she'd shake her head. But when she came to Mrs. Miller, who sat waiting for her, with eyes getting bigger and bigger, Alison stopped right in front of her, clapped her hand to her eyes, and dropped into a chair.

"What is it?" demanded Mrs. Miller, visibly frightened.

"I will na' say," was all we could get out of Alison. But presently she lifted her head, fixed her eyes on the door of the back parlor—Mrs. Miller's room, you know—and that queer, set look came back.

She got up, slowly, like a somnambulist, and walked in a queer, wooden way right up to the door and looked in, standing and swaying a little, and staring. Then she went right up to the bed, and again clapped her hands to her eyes, with a low cry, and came back to us, hastily. We all crowded around her.

"What is it, Alison? Do tell us! What did you see?"

But she shook her head darkly.

"We maun a' die in our beds—unless worse comes to us," she said. "What matters it where or when? Each one must dree his wierd."

But she did pause one moment by Mrs. Miller to whisper: "Ye'd be safer *higher up!*" Alison always had maintained that it was dangerous to sleep on the ground floor.

There was certainly a good deal of excitement among us.

We went and looked into the back parlor. I stepped in, and out again, quickly.

"Do you feel anything . . . queer?" I asked the little music teacher, who was actually shivering.

"I wouldn't go in there for anything!" she protested. "Mrs. Miller, *don't* sleep there. Come up and sleep with me."

Well, she did sleep upstairs that night, and the next day she left, furniture and all. She went to a hotel, and from there to a sanatorium—said her nerves were affected. And everywhere she went she spread reports that our house was haunted.

But as for us, we settled into peaceful ways again. I had a brilliant new wallpaper put on both parlors, opened the big doors wide, let in the sunshine, and kept the vases full of nasturtiums and coreopsis.

The little music teacher went away, but I soon had the rooms full again, and we went on as smoothly as before.

Some of the boarders tried to get Alison to tell what she saw, but she would only shake her head and smile, remarking that it took no great wisdom to say that folk died in their beds.

As the malign influence of Mrs. Miller wore off, and we had bright times as we did before, I think most of them concluded Alison had tried to frighten her off just because she didn't like her. I was quite willing they should think so.

Well! I breathed deep after that affair. Also I learned, if not humility, at least more caution. You see most people are easy. Even as a child I learned that. And most people are good—that is, well-intentioned. The harm they do is just by clumsiness—too many clumsinesses together. Then the meanest person I'd known, so far, was Father. Now I began to see, measuring him by Mrs. Miller, that Father wasn't *bad*, that is he did not try to do mischief. The trouble with Father was first being that kind of person, and then having married Mother. If he had married a different kind, such as Mrs. Miller, for instance, how different Father would have been. But she seemed to be really a bad person, seemed to like to do mischief for the fun of it.

When I counted up profit and loss I found that she had

just about paid for what she cost, in money. Except that one of the new boarders was not as permanent as the two who had quarrelled and left.

I was going to have a vacant room by the middle of August, and that was not an easy time to get another person in. Meantime I determined to make an extra effort in selecting a good one. Mother was to arrive home sometime in September.

Father had written home a few times—not often—and I had read his letters. What if it is a prison offense? It doesn't say anything against it in the Bible. Anyhow, it seemed right to me, and what I think is right I mean to do, law or no law. These laws people make, they unmake as fast as they make them—always having new ones and altering old ones, or repealing them. And they don't even pretend to have a revelation or anything. Besides, some are made on purpose by rich people, and the lawmakers paid to do it—I've read about that.

Well, anyway I read them, and he never said a word about that mortgage. If only I could keep him over there until I earned enough to pay it.

He didn't say anything about coming back, nor much about what he was doing, except visiting around among his cousins. There was no end to those cousins, and so far, he had only quarrelled with two and was still staying with the third. So I thought he'd be over there a long time.

Now if only I could get the right kind of person into that big front room—one of my best—before Mother came.

I had a pretty wide circle of acquaintances, and a lot of friends, too. I kept a list of them in a blank book, with descriptive notes (in cipher of course); and had their names dated by the calendar, with the unwritten note: "do something for." Anything would do, no matter how little, but people do love to be remembered. Every Sunday I'd look over my notes, as to that week's bunch, and take them flowers, or a library book to look at, or just stop and ask if I couldn't do an errand—anything.

I made a serious study of this list now, but everybody I knew either had a home, or was settled somewhere. Besides there wasn't one there who could fill just the place I had in mind.

Then, just happening to look out of the window, I saw someone turn in at Mrs. Gale's gate, and I had an inspiration. It was Mary Allen Windsor, the new woman minister who had just come to the little Universalist Church on Ash Street. I used to go there sometimes when Mr. Cutter was away, but I never liked their old minister; he looked like Noah, at least, if not Methuselah.

This one I'd heard once, the Sunday before, and liked immensely. Someone must have directed her to Mrs. Gale's because it was near, probably knew we were full, or was Mrs. Gale's friend. But I had a hope now.

She took a room there—poor Mrs. Gale always had vacancies, and I began my campaign.

First I went to her church, steadily, and thoroughly enjoyed it. Mr. Cutter was a nice man, and had always been a good friend to me, but he only preached religion, and this woman preached sense. I was tremendously pleased because, when you're doing things by force, as it were, all the time, it's nice to have something come natural. It was no effort at all to be fond of Mary A. Windsor. She was kind to me. That, I suppose, is part of a minister's business, but I wanted a lot more than that. I began to go to see her, running in with a few roses or a little dish of fruit or something, and never once staying too long. I asked questions about her sermons, and when she recommended books to read, I read them and asked more questions.

I brought some others to hear her, and with them, and the ones she had, I got up a little reading club at my house, once a week, and got her to drop in for a few minutes and advise us. She made a sort of special Bible class for us, and we had this other one on the side, in special reading. There was one book she had written herself, and we devoted ourselves to that. I got so I could quote from it extensively. That book was a great help, though I think I could have done it without it.

Club nights I asked her to dinner, and she did enjoy it— after the Gales'.

When it got to be nearly August I asked her if she could advise me about that room, if she knew anybody. "Won't you come and look at it," I said, "so you could recommend it."

"I suspect you of mercenary designs, Benigna," she said, and patted my shoulder. "But I'll look at it, certainly."

It was a very comfortable corner room, clean as a dish, the white curtains waving softly in the breeze, the bed in a sort of alcove that had a window in it too. The floor was bare, dark and shining, with a few rugs. There was a large writing table, in a good light, a big wastebasket, a low bookcase, a reading lamp. I had given a great deal of thought to that room. It was near the bathroom, and there was a little sink in it besides, with hot and cold water.

Mary Allen Windsor looked it over carefully. In her mind's eye, and in mine too, was that darkish room of Mrs. Gale's—big, but all full of furniture, with a spare little stand-uppish writing desk—sort of lady-in-the-parlor desk.

"I know a lady who would like it every much, Miss MacAvelly," she said. "And so do you, you designing young person. What do you charge for this room?"

It wasn't any more than Mrs. Gale's, and as soon as it was vacant she came over.

Then I drew a long sigh of relief. Here was a person of real dignity and position, one who could handle the conversation, push it or check it or turn it as she liked. I always wanted to do that, but of course I can't until I am a lot older. Perhaps never, if I keep on being so . . . so negative. But I like to see it done. And I felt sure Mother would like her. That was the main thing.

My purpose now was to study her tastes and wants, to make the place so comfortable she'd want to stay, and arrange the other boarders to suit her.

There was only one she seemd to really dislike, one of those patients of Dr. Bronson's, a sickly sort of person of course, being a patient, and showing a mean, critical spirit. Whatever the talk was he'd sit there with a superior little smile, and then say something calculated to make the other people feel small. At least it worked that way, and I don't believe it was an accident. Dr. Bronson said it was dyspepsia, but what difference did that make to us?

He played chess, and was very proud of it, used to play with the poor vegetarian gentleman and beat him, and be so hateful about it.

Miss Ayres' sister used to watch them a little, and he found she could play, and invited her to try a game with him. He beat her badly, and then made patronizing remarks about it, as to "the female mind," and so on.

I had never said that I could play or shown any interest in it, but now I did. I hung around until he said, "Well, young lady—do you think you can play chess?"

I told him I used to play with Father when I was quite a child.

"Aha! And did you beat him?"

"He beat me the most," I admitted.

"Beat you, did he? A father's privilege! Well, would you like to play with me?"

I could try, I said, and did try.

I played a weak sort of game, and he hardly gave his mind to it at all, but all of a sudden I took advantage of a weak point and mated him.

He was immensely astonished, and annoyed. But I said it was only that he had let me do it, accused him of encouraging me, and so on, and we tried again. This time he played better, but so did I, though still a quiet game, and the others gathered around to watch. He was awfully surprised that time, but I beat him again.

Mr. Wales, the vegetarian, began to get a little uproarious, he was so pleased; called me David, and his little champion, and things like that. Mrs. Coulter, that's Miss Ayres' sister, said that the female mind must vary somewhat. He was quite white about the lips by then, and had little dents round the corner of the nostrils, but he didn't say much—just asked me if I'd play again. I seemed willing to stop, suggested that perhaps he was tired, which made him madder than ever. I pleaded that I was tired, at which he accused me of cowardice, and finally we began again. This time, having watched his play and made up my mind as to methods, I beat him hard and quick, so quick he couldn't believe it.

He got up and went out of the room without a word, and they all praised me, but I said it was just because he was angry and didn't play his best. That was true enough.

They all kidded him about it a lot, particularly Mr. Wales, and urged him to play with me some more. At first he wouldn't, but I played with Mr. Wales, and he beat me, and then I played with Mrs. Coulter, and she beat me, so he thought it must have been an accident, and after a while he did try again. I beat him three straight games. After that they said he was in the infant class, and taunted him unmercifully. Whatever else came up, they would bring it back to chess, and pretty soon he left us.

I consulted with Miss Windsor about whom we should have next. I told her about Mother, and her temperament, and that in case Father's return was delayed I thought it would be such a good thing for Mother to have a nice congenial group of friends there.

"Or even if he does come back," I said, "I think Mother would enjoy earning some money of her own, don't you?"

"Every woman should earn her own money when it is possible," she said. And she gave her mind to it and suggested a young man in her church, who was putting himself through college.

"He can't pay much, but he is a dear fellow, and I know your mother would like him. Suppose you try. He can do a great deal about the place in winter, snow and coal and so on."

I thought it would be fine to have a nice young man in the house. With Mother at home it would be all right, and as for Peggy, I guessed I could manage.

He was waiting on table at a summer resort then, but he came just before college began. Now we had a nice family, and I waited with the utmost eagerness for Mother to come back.

She did arrive finally, and I declare I should hardly have known her. She was brown instead of pale; she was plump instead of thin; her eyes were bright. She'd had her teeth all put in order by Grandpa's dentist; there had never been money enough before.

Peggy looked blooming, of course. That was to be expected; but Mother was a joy.

She was a good deal overcome at first by the size of our family. I had written her from time to time, and so had Miss Ayres, to reassure her, but I don't think she had realized how many there were. But her room was all right, and Peggy's, and Alison was the picture of calm pride.

"Do I mind it, Mrs. MacAvelly?" she protested when Mother insisted it was too much for her. "Why should I mind cooking for a dozen, or two dozen, for that matter, any more than for four?"

"But the dishes, Alison, you have so many dishes to do afterwards."

"And what else should I do afterwards? I cannot cook the whole day long. No, Ma'am, I do not mind it, not if it is agreeable to you—on the same terms, that is, of course."

Mother was more than willing to ratify my arrangements, and wanted to give her more, but I dissuaded her. She was very dubious about going on with it, but I begged her to try it for a while anyway.

"It'll take up your mind, Mother dear," I said, "while Father is away. And I believe you'll like it."

I had guessed pretty well, but even I had not imagined just how much she would like it. You see some of them were old friends of hers, and the rest soon became new ones. The boy, Robert Aylesworth, she took to her heart at once. He was an orphan it appeared, and he did enjoy being mothered, and was so tender and polilte to her it did my heart good to watch him.

And Mary Allen Windsor—I *was* so pleased! She took to dear little Mother as I hoped she would, and Mother simply laid hold of her like a long-neglected vine rushing up a congenial trellis. Father wasn't a very good trellis.

I don't mean that Mother was offensively devoted—not a bit of it—but she seemed to find just the kind of strength and stimulus she needed. It was exactly what I had hoped, and better. Mother was busy all the morning, fussing about trying to make things more pleasant for her guests. There was time enough for visiting, afternoons, or for pretty work such as she loved to do, with nice people to talk to. In the evening we had games, and Mother would play for us, or some of the others would. Robert Aylesworth could sing, just hymns and college songs and such—a nice baritone voice. And we played whist. Mother did love whist so, and she played a good game when Father was not there to intimidate her.

There was only one thing I was afraid of now. That was that Mother would save up enough to send for Father. I had never told her how much of a profit there was, and Alison never let on how much she made. Trust Alison for keeping quiet. It was easy of course to keep on with the accounts myself. She was glad to have me do it, and as I took in the money and paid the bills I could hand over what I liked.

There was some profit for her, of course, really more than she expected, for Mrs. Gale had long since persuaded her that keeping boarders spelled ruin. But she had to clothe herself and Peggy out of it. I told her I took out so much a week for my own services, and now Peggy helped a little and made her own pocket money.

If I thought Mother was accumulating any I always urged some new supplies—linen, or dishes, or something. But the real surplus that did accumulate I kept to myself—literally and metaphorically.

﹋ CHAPTER TEN

Things went on wheels for a while, with our boarding house. Before Thanksgiving we were running smoothly, with some extra table boarders. Table boarders are a great help. We had six, young men mostly, two older ones.

Of course after Mother came back we could have men, and they seemed to like to come. We only charged $5.00 a week for table board—and $2.50 of that was profit. Mother got $5.00 a week from the six, and I saved $10.00. With that, and $30.00 a week kept back from the previous income, my private safe got fuller and fuller, and I got more and more excited. I'd been paying the interest on that mortgage all along out of my own salary—you see it was only $80.00 a year—about $1.50 a week. And I saved as much as I could out of the rest, and counted ahead carefully (we had to buy a lot of coal in the summer—that kept Mother pretty close, though I paid for some), and before Christmas I had it!

Thirty dollars a week for thirty-two weeks, plus $10.00

a week for twelve weeks—$1,080. My! I did draw a long breath!

A thousand dollars inside of a year! It was better than I had hoped. I'd had extra expenses, too, but there was my own $3.50 to draw on—that made $112; and with what Grandpa left for me to live on all summer—I really had the thousand!

To pay that mortgage—to really pay it, get that dreadful thing with my name on it back in my hands and burn it—I tell you, that was a joy!

I hadn't realized until it was done what a strain I'd been living under. I really had worked awfully hard—gardening, and marketing, and being waitress and chambermaid for eight, besides ourselves. Peggy helped, of course, after she came, and the extra "mealers" came; but I certainly had my hands full.

It was a real Achievement; and as there wasn't a soul on earth I could tell about it, I enjoy writing it down.

It wasn't so dreadful after all, but pretty close calculating. I used to get up at 5:30, have my highly gymnastic scrub-bath, and come down stealthily to the kitchen. Alison got up early, too, and I'd have a glass of milk and a cracker to start on. Then an hour in the garden—lovely work that was, though pretty damp; everything so bright and beady, and smelling so good. You can do a lot in a garden in an hour a day.

Then I'd dust the parlors and set the table—we had to have a 7:30 breakfast on account of those boarders. By 9:00 the last one was fed and the room clean; and I'd had my breakfast sort of casually, waiting on them as needed.

By 10:30 I had the rooms in order upstairs, sweeping two a day usually; and from 10:30 to 11:30 was marketing. I didn't have to go far, fortunately, and of the keepable groceries I always had a good stock in advance. Between 11:30 and 12:15 I just *rested*—reading or sewing—and it felt good. Then the table was to be set for our early lunch; those schoolteachers had to have it at 12:30, and by 2:00 P.M. the dining room was clear and left dark and cool for the afternoon.

Afternoons I had quite an easy time; only there are always things to do in a house. But I did the main work before lunch.

And I went to bed early, religiously, by 9:00 most nights, and got eight hours' sleep. It was real sleep, too. I used to go to bed so happy—because the Secret Hoard was rolling up from week to week.

By Christmas week the thing was done—*Done*—and I felt like Alexander the Great!

Considering what world to conquer next, I spent quite a time in thinking and planning.

There was a very tempting world next door—Mrs. Gale's house. I wanted—oh, how I wanted—to get Mrs. Gale out, and my mother in!

Only to do that, and to do other things I wanted to away from home, I must have an Accomplice. Failing an Accomplice, I must reduce my ideas of boardinghouse profit, hire a mere manager, or leave it to Mama, with much less of an income—less, that is, than I could have made by doing it myself. I planned it all out on paper carefully.

This boardinghouse business wasn't *my* business—it was Mother's. I had already accomplished my cherished Purpose. Father was gone, Mother was happy, and my Crime was obliterated—I'd torn up the deed.

I wanted to leave the boardinghouse business so that it would be easy for Mother—plus Alison—to keep it up. Naturally Peggy could not be counted upon—she might go off most any time.

The question was: Ought I to stay, to push the business and keep an eye on Peggy, or could I begin now to launch out and do the other things I wanted to?

I watched Peggy. Pretty—prettier—prettiest; she certainly was the most fascinating thing. All the he-boarders seemed to think so, and their friends thought so, too—and the young men of the church—both churches, Mr. Cutter's and Mrs. Windsor's, and lots besides.

Before New Year's I made up my mind. My sister's happiness in life might depend on my staying at home now. If I weren't there, there was no knowing whom she might marry, and there was room for considerable choice.

Also, if I stayed another year, and took in the World next door, and ran it myself, I might with perfect honesty, or at least, with *tolerable* honesty, accumulate quite a little money. So far as I know it is *always* useful to have a little money, unless it is gold money or a large necklace of silver, and you are about to drown.

Accomplice—or Assistant?

I decided on an Assistant—I was afraid I couldn't find, or make, an Accomplice quite yet.

I laid it out like this:

"Some day Peggy will marry; I shall be away on Enterprises of my own, and Mother will be alone. I want to leave her so completely entrenched in a smooth-running, well-paying house, that she can't spoil it by too much kindness. She ought to have a capable, stern, hard-headed businesswoman to keep her up.

"Then if my dear Mrs. Windsor will only stay, I do believe she could hold her own even if the worst happened." (That was if Father came back and told her to stop it.)

So I began to study my list of friends and acquaintances that I had all set down with bits of description. Right there I began to find out something which I have been finding out ever since: the real smart, capable people are *busy*—you can't find them lying around loose. And the ones who are disengaged, so to speak, are pretty generally useless.

"Man or woman?" I said to myself.

"Men that amount to anything are all busy. Young ones are sure to leave, if at all clever.

"Women—young ones—are likely to marry. Old ones are mostly occupied if worth anything. Left-overs are no good."

Then I settled on this: if I could find a youngish middle-aged woman with an Incumbrance, say a child—or even two—who was smart enough to keep all the accounts straight and not let Mother . . . and then and there I stopped short and began to reconsider.

All this propping up Mother from the outside was

uncertain in the extreme. If she couldn't, she couldn't, that was all. But if she could . . .

Then I resolved to put in a solid year, making everything as strong and safe as I could, and sort of educating Mother into some degree of independence. I counted on Mrs. Windsor to help, and she did, steadily, without seeming to realize it.

You see Mother liked her so much that it was easy. She began to read her books and came in and sat with our class, and then she and Mrs. Windsor would read other books together.

Then Mrs. Windsor, all of her own idea, got Mother interested in some of her protegés and projects, and I could fairly see her grow. I began to think I hadn't done Mother justice. There are people who never amount to anything when they are with the wrong influence, and who come out surprisingly under others.

Dr. Bronson did Mother a world of good. He was a bachelor, and an old friend; she always used to brighten up when he came, and Robert and the other boys were all devoted to Mother.

So I turned my whole mind on the next move. That was to get Jenny Gale a job, a good job, and then . . .

This was not very hard, with so many people to ask. I had quite a good talk with Dr. Bronson first.

"Mrs. Gale doesn't look very well, does she?" I began. He agreed that she didn't.

"Don't you think it would be really better for her if Jenny could do the work she liked, and support her mother—or help to?"

"It would be a great deal better, Ben. She worries herself sick over her work and never gets ahead any. And Jenny worries too, because she hates it. But what are we going to do about it?"

I meditated hard, as if I'd never thought of it before.

"If we could persuade Mrs. Gale to stop . . ." I said.

"She won't—says she must keep a home for Jenny."

"Yes, well, if Jenny had a real good chance, a job that would pay her well . . ."

"Even then her mother's tied up with the business. I don't see how she could stop."

I looked up at him, and smiled.

"See here, Dr. Bronson," I said, "which would you rather do—honest!—eat at Mrs. Gale's table or at ours?"

He smiled, too, and refused to answer the question. But I knew well enough.

"May I tell you a secret," I said, "that you'll never, never tell?"

"That's what doctors are for," he answered, "to keep secrets. I've had so many that I've forgotten them by the hundred."

Then I told him, ingeniously, what I was sure he knew already, that I was doing all this for Mother's sake, and that I wanted her to have it all sound and safe—even if Father came back.

"Don't you think she would be better off, with boarders, even if he did come?" I asked.

His face hardened the minute I mentioned Father. "Of course she would," he replied briefly.

"Well now, see here," I said, and showed him some calculations I had made.

Mrs. Gale's house rented for $75 a month. It had twelve bedrooms—counting the doctor's back parlor and the maid's—ten lettable ones. Of course, she kept one for herself and Jenny, and never had her nine full at once. Also a lot of people went off without paying.

"Ten boarders," I showed him, "averaging $10.00 a week, is $5,200 a year. That's the biggest possible income. The rent is $900. The fuel and light—say $200. One girl for waitress and chambermaid—about $300. That's $1,400. Then if I pay $4.00 a week apiece for food (of course I wasn't going to, but I didn't mean to tell him everything) it's $2,080—plus $1,400—that's $3,480. Take that from $5,200 and it leaves $1,720. You see that leaves a margin of $1,720 Take out $150 for fuel, etc., and it's $1,570. And if I lost equal to one boarder all the time, there'd still be over a thousand."

He studied it carefully. "There's something wrong here, Ben—there must be. This is too good to be true. You've left out something."

"Of course I have," I agreed. "I've left out the cook—and the manager—and the furniture. Now Alison can cook for twenty or thirty, she says so. You see she has no other work. And dear Mother could run two houses as well as one—you'd all eat over there, of course; and the whole furnishing, put it at $500, would only be $150 a year, at 10 percent. I'd soon buy it. Really Dr. Bronson, it can be done.

"I notice that you keep *your* house full," he admitted.

"Yes—and we haven't any losses because they all pay in advance. It's just as cheap for them."

"I believe she could do it, Ben," he said, "with you behind her. You're a pretty smart young woman. I've always said so." And he gave me a friendly little shake. "So what is your proposition, little Miss Manager?"

"Why, I'm kind of ashamed to make it," I told him, "but it's this. You see, Jennie tells me how things are, and I've planned it this way. Mrs. Gale has signed the lease, of course, up to next May, and she's owing for all that coal—she's only paid for three tons, and there's four left. And I suppose she'd want something for 'the good will of the business.' "

He smiled at that. He knew as well as I did—better, really—how little good will there was left in Mrs. Gale's business.

"If you'd stay right on, at the same rate," I said rather sheepishly—I knew he was paying about $900 a year for his two big rooms and board, $17.00 a week I think it was— "and if you felt you could trust us enough to advance it for—" he smiled reassuringly as I hesitated, "for six months, then I'd have something to pay off Mrs. Gale."

"Why, my dear child, I'd pay it for a year," he said cordially. "And trust you for twenty more in case anything happened to your undertaking. Tell me when you're ready and I'll give you a check or cash, as you prefer."

"Jennie's job is the first thing," I suggested rather gloomily.

"That won't be hard, I think. Jenny Gale is a pretty smart young woman," he continued. "We'll find her something."

I did not tell him that I still had Mother to persuade, but I felt sure that would not take long. She was fond of Jenny, and so was Mrs. Windsor, and they sympathized with her efforts to get a position. Mrs. Windsor helped a lot—I believe she really found the right place at last.

I put it to Mother on the ground of being such a chance for dear Jenny; and then that it would be Mrs. Gale's salvation.

"Dr. Bronson says it's worry and nothing else that ails her. He says if she could have a rest and no care she'd be a well woman."

When Mother hesitated over the risk, I went over the figures with her—still keeping that $4.00 estimate on food, and showed her that possible $1,570—or even $1,070 clear profit.

And, to finish, I began to say how all our boarders loved the food here, and loved her, and how Dr. Bronson would prefer our table, that he fairly suffered at Mrs. Gale's, and she was just about converted.

We had a talk with Alison, all three together. I had already spoken to her about it, and she was more than willing. It meant more money for her, too, and she delighted in her enlarged scale of cooking.

Mrs. Gale was the hardest to move. She complained about her debts; I assured her we would take them all. She spoke of the furniture, fairly dwelt upon it, until I asked her what she thought it was really worth. She said, after figuring on it a long while, perhaps $1,200.

You see, she had had very little of her own at first, and had had to buy from time to time. She got her things second-hand, and at auction sales—it was a poor lot, and old. There was hardly any real silver, and the bed and table linen was pretty well worn out. When I offered to pay her $300 down, and 10 percent a year on the rest until I could buy it, she was much impressed.

She, too, spoke, rather half-heartedly, of the "good will of the business," but even Mother knew better than that.

"Of course, Mrs. Gale, that is right," she agreed. "Just show us the annual profit and we shall be obliged to pay you on that basis."

"Well, Mrs. MacAvelly, I haven't the face to claim any profit," the poor woman said. "I've worked like a slave and so has Jenny, but beyond keeping a roof over our heads, and clothes on our backs, there's nothing to show for it. You've done better, I know, but then you own your house —that makes a big difference, a very big difference. I don't advise you to take my house," she went on. "In conscience I can't advise you to. It's a hard house to heat, and to keep clean . . ."

It took quite a good deal of persuading all around, but presently Mrs. Gale was out and we were in, with the rent to pay and the furniture to buy and Dr. Bronson's advance to begin it with.

We were soon running full houses, with a smart young woman to keep the Gale house clean, and Alison getting extremely important over her cooking—and her increased income. She never had had enough to do for us. Alison had real capacity.

But life is a complicated thing, I find. No sooner had I got the business going smoothly, with a chance of paying off everything, and even getting some new furniture by next winter, than things began to happen at home.

I had kept an eye on Peggy, of course; but there was one thing I never thought of—that was anybody's falling in love with me.

It was that nice Robert Aylesworth. He was just the dearest boy—I was as fond of him as could be, but as for marrying him—oh, never!

Of course I did not mean to marry at all. I'd seen enough of it. Besides, how could I marry, and be Benigna Machiavelli!

I was planning for such a number of things to do in life, one after the other. Most people seem to me to spend their lives in coops. The boys run into an office and the girls run into a house, headlong, and there they sit as long as they live, in coops.

I wanted Adventures—and I meant to have them. All these preliminaries were only to do my duty by my family first—then I was going to be off.

As for Robert, I had been hoping, distinctly hoping, that he'd fall in love with Peggy as all the others did. He was so sweet with Mother, and he wasn't *over* ambitious. I thought perhaps he'd be willing to live at home and back up Mother in the business.

With that view I had confided in him a little, just a little; and the foolish boy was quite impressed with what I'd been doing. I told him it wasn't anything, that housekeeping was a thing any woman ought to be good at.

"Maybe they ought to be, but they are not," said Robert, and he proceeded to follow me about and invite me to things, until I had to notice it.

It was quite exciting, in a way. Though I did not mean to marry, I had no objection to being asked. And then I found there was a certain satisfaction in having somebody always considering one's wishes and doing nice little things for one.

As soon as spring opened and I began to work in my enlarged garden, there was Robert, being so practically helpful that I couldn't refuse him. A man is a very useful thing after all—when he's willing. I had always thought of them chiefly as Obstacles, my experience being rather limited.

Also I found that with this nice boy always about, talking of his ideals and hopes and things (he didn't propose, you see; he couldn't because he was only a student, but he wanted to), I began to feel a sort of change in my own mind. It was a funny, quicksandy sort of feeling. Here I was, just starting out in life—shall be twenty-one before very long now—it seems a lifetime since I began this record. Well—it is my lifetime, practically. Then right at the beginning, just as I was ready to break loose and Go—here was this nice boy offering me a coop. The worst of it was that coops began to look almost attractive!

"This won't do," I said. "This will *not* do! Women have been known to lose their heads in a case like this. Sit down, and have it out with yourself, Benigna Machiavelli, before it's too late! Do you want to marry Robert Aylesworth, or do you not?"

Then I answered myself sharp and clear: "I do not!" And yet there was something that wasn't satisfied, something that worried me, it felt so . . . uncertain.

"Can't I handle a thing like this?" I demanded. "Am I, with all the determination of years of planning, to be changed by the first nice boy who shows he is attracted to me?"

I took a whole evening to myself, in my attic room, and plenty of paper, and faced the thing carefully. I had no long life of experience to look back on for suggestion, and no person I cared to ask about it. Besides, if I did, they'd probably think it was a good thing—there was nothing against Robert. I knew Mother would be delighted . . . No, I had to think it out.

And then, if I had no experience of my own, I had all the world's—in books. They generally give in, I notice, unless something intervenes. I noticed that when it was a man who was sort of drifting in a direction he did not wish to go, his friends always told him there was no safety but in flight.

"He who fights and runs away, lives to fight another day." I made up my mind to take no chances—I would fly.

I determined to trust Peggy with the accounts. That would give her a sense of responsibility; and (this seemed particularly wise) to get Robert to help her with them. I showed Robert first—he was splendid in mathematics—binding him to secrecy, of course.

"It's for Mother," I told him. "She can market and manage

the place beautifully, but she has no head for figures. Now I want Peggy to get interested in this for her own sake and—I'll trust you with this, too—I'm awfully afraid Peggy will marry the wrong one. No, I won't say a word more—but I wish you'd . . . brother her a little."

He flushed to his hair and looked at me. That word "brother" almost upset him. But I was calm. "All girls need brothers," I said, "I'm sure I'm glad of all the brothering you've given me." I didn't stop at that—not for a minute—because he looked as if he were about to say things. I went right on. "Now I'm going to tell you my real Secret, since you seem so kind and interested." And I told him something about Father, and how there was more money in the business than Mother knew, and that I wanted to save it for her.

"As far as you know you'll be here until you're through college, won't you?" I asked. "If we keep on with boarders?"

"Indeed, I will," he agreed eagerly. "And oh, I do hope you'll keep on."

Then I said that I felt I had too much to do, which was quite true in a way, and that I thought Peggy could do this with help. He could be a sort of auditor, and help Peggy save the money.

Peggy was delighted with the conspiracy. She didn't want Father to come home any more than I did. She'd never had such nice times in her life.

We started a savings account, in my name, though I didn't mention the amount of cash I had concealed upstairs—there's no need of telling everything. They thought I'd done perfect wonders already in getting the Gale house to running profitably.

I had fixed it so that poor bunch of furniture and stuff would be all paid for in a year's time, and some left over, besides buying coal and various things. And I'd "kept back part of the price"—for salary. I'd earned it.

But they had a couple of hundred to put in the bank, and a chance of a handsome addition from then on. Peggy knew as well as I did about Mother's weakness of heart, and was as willing to connive as I had hoped.

"Let her have some profit, of course, and let it grow a little—but see that she spends it, won't you, Peggy?"

Peggy said she would. She had a bigger salary, too, now, and that pleased her, but she wasn't a good saver.

I told them that it would be cheaper to let Alison do the marketing, if they could persuade Mother. "Give her $2.50 a week, per each. If she wants more, she'll say so."

Robert sat with us several evenings, while I helped her get used to it. I told him that I felt so safe about my sister when he was with her.

"Wouldn't it be a shame," I said, "if a nice pretty girl like that was to go and marry anybody who would make her unhappy? Of course, it may not be so. But you'll be doing me a kindness, truly, if you will be as nice to Peggy as you can."

It wasn't any hardship to be nice to Peggy, and then Robert was nice to everybody.

Then I told Peggy that I knew she didn't care a bit for Robert, but I had reason to believe that he had a Disappointment, and that he was an orphan anyway, and had no sister, and I thought all that she and Mother did for him was really a great comfort to the boy.

"Perhaps he's having too much 'sister' now," she said. Peggy is not a fool—nowhere near it. But I looked blank and went on talking.

Having got that all going nicely, I had a heart-to-heart talk with Mrs. Windsor. She always did me good. I found that she was quite happy there, and meant to stay. I'd thought she would, and I felt safe about Mother while she was there.

"There's only one thing that worries me," I said. "If Father comes back I'm afraid he'll make Mother give it all up. And then she'll just settle down and be the frail invalid she was before. Mother needs people. She needs friends, and young folks around, and something going on. You'd back her up, wouldn't you, Mrs. Windsor?"

"Your mother owns this house, I understand?"

"Yes, and she's signed the lease for the other one."

"And your father, so far, has not . . . well, has not been very successful in business?"

"No, not ever—just a spurt now and then, and then we'd get in debt and be poor for ever so long."

"Your mother has a perfect right to carry on this work if she chooses. I shall certainly do all I can to strengthen her determination if necessary."

Then I told Mother I thought I needed a vacation, and would she mind if I went to see Grandpa for a while. She was very willing—she had worried over my working so hard for so long.

Grandpa was willing, too, and I went off at once, with a suitcase and a little handbag, and hidden away in a little oilskin bag that hung around my neck, $500.

Grandpa would do as a sort of springboard.

CHAPTER ELEVEN

As I look over my notes for that year, whole books of them, I realize that any true autobiography is too long. Why, you live *every day,* and things happen, real interesting things. Also there are so many people—I keep a record of them, you see—and people who are more amusing and surprising all the time.

Of course if you just stay at home, as most girls do, all the people you know are family and schoolmates and church people, and afterwards the ones you meet "socially." But that never satisfied me. I had all those classified quite early, and all the rest of the world was left to get acquainted with.

I had determined on a wander year—maybe more. I wanted to "see life," as it says in the books; not that silly get-drunk-and-play-cards behavior that is called "seeing life," nor yet the dinner-opera-dancing kind. Neither of these seemed like life to me.

I wanted to see how life *worked,* to learn how to run things and watch people doing it. There at Grandpa's I rested awhile. I found that I was really quite tired. That Robert affair had bothered me more than I imagined such a thing could. Not that I loved him—I could see easily enough that it wasn't *that*. I didn't want to give up my life for him. I didn't want to give up anything for him. It was just that he was such a nice fellow and it is so pleasant to have somebody to care such a lot about you. It's no wonder so many girls marry whomever asks them, especially if they are not really satisfied at home. But I had other fish to fry, very different ones, and didn't propose to have my frying cut off short before it began.

So I sat down at Grandpa's, in my big cool corner bedroom with the four windows, and made a chart of my life. It was a good deal like an ancient map—chopped off short with "unexplored region," or "circling unknown sea," but it was clear enough as far as it went.

"Twenty-one," I said, "shall be in a couple of months. Healthy and strong.

"Present capacities:

    a. Housekeeping, managing, purchasing.

    b. Cooking, catering, serving.

    c. Sewing, designing, dressmaking.

    d. Stenography and typing.

Education—ordinary.

Special talents: Self-control, understanding people; knowing how to manage them.

Purposes in life:

    A. To grow. To be as big as I can—in every sort of way.

    B. To use my powers to straighten things as far as I can."

I was very certain about A, completely clear indeed, and determined; B was sort of misty. So far I had just done little things that came up, and there always seemed to be something that needed fixing.

"Now then," I wrote down, "how can I grow the most and the fastest in the next five years—or six—or seven?"

You see, I had not made up my mind *inflexibly* not to marry; I just didn't mean to if I could help it, and certainly not until I had done a lot of other things first. So I planned for five years, definitely. Twenty-six is quite young enough to "settle down," as they call it.

"I'll get a job in an office, just for a starter," I said. "Get an idea of real business methods." That I put to Grandpa confidentially—but I guess I'll tell about the plan first. It was a tentative plan. I knew well enough how things change on your very hands, but I meant to have a settled purpose.

"Here is a lifetime," I said solemnly. "I'll lay it out as if I were not to marry—that's safest. And the other end is the place to plan from.

"Age. What do I want to have about me, and behind me, when I'm old?"

Then I'd sit back in my rocker and look out at the big trees and soft changing shadows on the grass, and *think,* think hard about Age.

There were plenty of old people to think about. I knew a lot of them, mostly as grandmas and grandpas.

Health was the main thing. To keep well always so as to be pink and straight and cheerful at seventy—that was certainly common sense.

I remembered Mrs. Windsor's mother, who came to see her at our house once, and that minister from Nebraska who preached in Dr. Cutter's church one summer, and the big surgeon from Germany that Dr. Bronson had to visit him once. Splendid old people, not crabbed or feeble or foolish.

Then besides health, any old person has to have some money. If they haven't, they're just poor relations, and are put upon.

Of course the old men generally do, but the old women generally don't. A grandpa is a person to be considered on account of what he may give you—before or after; but a grandma is only to be considered according to whether you love her or not, apparently.

"I shall have my own money, and enough of it," I determined, "married or single. And I shall have a home—a home of my own, not just somebody else's home that I keep house in." And I thought of another old person I knew, a relative of Jennie Gale's on her father's side, who had a beautiful place in the country, and people loved to visit her. She had crowds of jolly young folks and various kinds of people. She never was lonesome, that I could see, though an "old maid."

Health, money, home—what next?

Friends! Now that is the most important of all, almost. Friends are the richest kind of riches. I've noticed old folks mourn because of the "dropping off" of their friends, their "old friends." One would think that friends were strictly limited to one crop, like brothers and sisters. I mean to plant mine in succession, like green peas and sweetcorn, so I'll always have ripe ones. Why, that relation of Jenny's was simply worshipped by some of those young things, boys as well as girls, and she always had middle-aged ones too.

Health, money, home, friends. How about Family? That I wouldn't plan for. If it came, it would come. I was planning for life without it, so's to be on the safe side. There's a certain definite proportion of unmarried women. Funny that young women never plan accordingly!

What next? What *kind* of an old woman did I want to be?

Here was where that big A, "To Grow," came in. I wanted above all things to be a *worthy* person. To be a plus and not a minus. Not to spend my days wanting things and hanging on to people, and being hurt or pleased or disappointed by the things they did. I wanted to be a *wise* person—wise and able. One that other folks would come to for advice and help, and not be disappointed. Sort of, "Oh, we'll ask Benigna Machiavelli—she'll tell us!"

Of course I knew amiable old ladies, and awfully kind nice ones, but they didn't know much about Life—only about recipes and patterns and their special notions about babies.

Now my idea was to enlarge my circle of experience as widely as possible, and to keep on enlarging it. So I meditated very deeply on how much could be put into that five years, and more, if I had more free to use in the same way.

Languages. I'd always been good at languages, such as we had in school. I had a background of Latin, and the beginnings of German and French. One thing I determined on was to spend several summers abroad and learn different languages on the spot.

This was extremely interesting to lay out.

"French," I said. "Paris, of course. Not as a tourist—they'd talk English to me. Just *be* there; be left on my own resources. Get board in a nice refined French family, and get work in a French shop, a business office. Yes, that will be best. Try more than one. Can go over as companion or nursemaid. Better get nursemaid's training. Need a lot of Personal Recommendations, that's one thing sure. Get them. Can come back the same way. Can always take a vacation when I need it. See to it that I have some money with me, always."

Then I'd hug my little $500, the nucleus of all my further fortunes.

Danger? That was another point to consider. If I were going out like this, all about the earth at random, and especially if I had money with me, there would always be an element of danger.

It was tremendously exciting to plan for that. One thing I determined on—to have Disguises! I must learn to "make up" my face. It would be good to take a little while on the stage perhaps, behind the scenes, and learn a bit about that. And I put down: "Lady's maid experience—situation with actor."

I got up at this point, I remember, and looked at myself in the glass. Now as I've said before, I was not beautiful nor distinguished looking. I suppose a discriminating describer, like those novelists, could have seen a lot in my face, but most people didn't seem to. Still I was young and fresh and not wholly unattractive—there was Robert to show that.

Then I had a perfectly *lovely* idea.

"I'll fix up to look older!" I said. "A lot older! There are plenty of old ladies planning to look young—I'll learn how to look thirty or forty! Oh, what fun! Then it'll be so jolly to pop out, as a young woman, when I want to." And I determined on that actor/lady's maid arrangement as really useful.

"I'll have a whole series of names," I said. "I'll have a lot of costumes. I'll learn enough trades to get work anywhere! I'll go anywhere I please on earth—!"

It was tremendously exciting.

When I got my tentative plan well drawn out it was like an old-fashioned game I saw when I was little, where there was a kind of winding maze, with the "House of Happiness" in the middle. You spun a top, I think, a hexagonal one, numbered, and moved counters to that number. My plan was much clearer and better. There was a great circle and then inner ones—and in the middle was that Splendid Old Age I was planning for. In the inner circles there were not many things to do, because naturally you don't expect old people to do as much as young ones, and then, also naturally, I couldn't specify very much that far ahead. But in the outer ones!

I got a census list of Occupations and marked in red all the ones I'd really like to try. There were a lot. Then I put the difficult and highly skilled ones well in toward the middle—things I'd like to do when I was thirty, when I was forty, when I was fifty—it was tremendously exciting to put things down on the fifty line.

There was College President, Position in the City Government, Owner of a System of Hotels, Head of a Great School, Manufacturer with Model Factories—things like that. And from each of those, lines ran back to the wider rings where I had arranged the successive smaller undertakings by which I proposed to lead up to the big ones.

The outside ring was where I stood now, planning for my next job. I could see at the outset that every one of them would help with the others. Then I said, "Wait a minute—which of these lines is going to bring me in touch with people on top? Big People—aristocrats—I want to know all kinds."

It wasn't done in a minute, this chart. I stayed a month at Grandpa's, resting and thinking.

This aristocracy idea was not easy to handle at first, but I went at it from the top end, as I usually do.

"Wanted: easy familiarity with people of the best manners." I fixed on the English aristocracy, at least to begin with—and laid out this line of advance. "Last step, trusted and friendly companion with elderly and perhaps eccentric English woman who has fine houseparties. Back of that, high recommendations from lesser English person. Back of that, introduction by American friend, with very high recommendation."

From there it was to go easy backwards. Two careful summers abroad ought to make a good linguist and courier; four ocean trips as nurse and companion ought to command very favorable acquaintance and esteem. I just hugged myself as I thought of those voyages.

It was easy to see that I must do the lowest grade things first, pile up such experiences quickly and under other names, and go on to the larger ones. I should have to cut loose from home altogether, that was clear. I could go to a distant city, have a settled address, and write such letters as I chose— meanwhile doing things.

Very well! I had a nice talk with Grandpa, earnest and innocent as you please. I told him how happy Mother was, that she had evidently inherited from him a real talent for large management, and that I felt sure it would make another woman of her—even if Father came back. I told him that I had enjoyed getting it started ever so much, but that I realized my limitations and wanted very much to learn more.

"Don't you think a girl ought to have some real knowledge of business?" I asked him. "No matter what happens to her? Now I wish you'd help me in this, Grandpa; I want to get a position in a business office. Not here where anybody'd know me, but in a Western city. I want to board and work by myself for a while—I think it will do me good. Won't you make believe I'm a boy, Grandpa, and help get me a place, with some firm you know about, perhaps? I'd like to take the first with your knowledge and advice."

Grandpa was not so old-fashioned but that he could see the sense of this idea; and he liked my appealing to him in that way.

I wanted to do this because it would be the easiest way to straighten it out with Mother. Once clean gone, she'd have to get used to it, that's all.

Grandpa hemmed and hawed a good deal, but he came around. He had a good opinion of my abilities, you see, and a great respect for business training.

I rather hated to start in with even this much assistance, but I knew I *could* have done it half a dozen ways—if I'd had to.

But this seemed wise to begin with, and Grandpa himself wrote to Mother of my laudable desire to enlarge my experience, and that he thought it was a good thing.

He had an old friend in a big firm in Chicago, and they gave me a trial, a cheap little chance at only ten dollars a week, as a typist and stenographer.

"You can't live on that, child," said Grandpa. "Here, you must take some money with you for an emergency. And be sure you keep me posted as to how you get on." He made me take fifty dollars. "That's enough to come back with," he said. And I told him I should return it out of my savings.

Oh! Oh! How splendid I felt when I set out for Chicago, all by myself, just twenty-one that very week! I don't suppose Prosper Le Gai was any gayer than I was that day.

I went to one of those young-woman homes at first— that was for experience. And I got it. While sampling, I went to one after another, all I could get into, in Chicago, and learned and learned and learned.

One notebook is about those "Homes." I got acquainted with the young women there, lots of them, and that was especially useful. All I'd found out with my school friends was corroborated here.

It is so easy to make friends that I perfectly marvel at the stupidity of those who don't. Sympathy, kindness, patience, interest, and service, if possible—but even without service the others do it. You have to keep yourself in the background, of course, but I was an adept at that. Not that I was unselfish, or that horrid bottomless gulf they call "selfless," no indeed! I was brimful and running over with plans and purposes all my own, but they included friends—depended on them. One may have a large and lively Self and yet keep it in decent restraint while other people let theirs play about.

At the office I learned some things, and gained what I

wanted—speed and precision in my work, and some knowledge of business habits and manners. At the end of a month I changed. My five years was all too short to waste much time on these preliminaries.

Then things began to move. I kept my house address at the cheapest of the Homes, and started in on a career of industry of the most varied character.

Plain of dress and quiet of manner, with my serious face and steady eyes, I got jobs without much difficulty. There were times when I didn't, times when I stood in line for hours, waited about doorways, was briefly interviewed, and superciliously turned down by employers; learned, by practical experience, what it is to be out of work.

I was healthy, I was courageous, I had no one dependent on me. I had my enormous plans to keep me interested, and I had always my secret hoard in its little oil-silk bag. But at that it was hard enough.

For those others who had nothing but what they earned, who often had other mouths to feed, who had neither health nor high purpose to keep them going, nor any reserve fun at all, it was just purgatory. I've got a notebook about *that*.

I joined Unions, and was discharged for it. I went to Settlement Clubs and Classes and learned a lot. Then it seemed a good chance to start in on the child question, and after helping a bit, gratuitously, in the Settlement Nursery, I got a regular place in one.

That was meat and drink to me. I had always liked babies, but not . . . well, not to lose my heart entirely to just one. This roomful appealed to me very much. The head nurse was an extremely capable one, and taught me a great deal. I put in a month in this kind of nursery work, and then thought I'd increase my experience in that line.

By the good offices of the Settlement people I got a sort of assistant nursemaid place in a rich family, and had all I wanted of that in two weeks. But I made the acquaintance of a very good lady's maid there, who became cheerfully confidential and told me about her various places, mistresses, and duties.

I answered advertisements and got a maid's place, at low wages, stating that I had worked in other lines before; and then I began to learn new things, very fast.

Why do not people realize that you cannot know life if you stay always on one level? Why, the average woman knows only her own kind of people. She may travel around the world, and never learn as much as she would in traveling *up and down a bit* in her own city.

I had been associating with office women, shop women, factory women, and nurse women. Now I did not associate, in the ordinary sense, with rich women, but I had to learn about them—I couldn't help it.

With my hair depressingly low and plain, with the regulation dress of my "class," and with the manners of the same, which I studied and practised with joy, I don't believe Mother would have known me at the first look.

As to make-up, I began to find out about that even as a lady's maid, and was ready to try for the position with an actor.

I wrote nice letters home. The address changed now and then, and I told chatty stories of my various boardinghouses, and people I met. Also I wrote much of their affairs, only Mother would sometimes protest. "You don't tell us enough about *yourself,* Benigna. Are you still in the same place, or have you changed again? I do wish you would come back."

Grandpa was much annoyed that I should change about, but I wrote him nice letters too.

"You see, dear Grandfather," I'd tell him, just as fully and courteously as if it was necessary, "I am not doing this because I have to, but to gain knowledge of life first-hand. It is hard for a woman to get this. After marriage I should have no chance for such attempts—now is my time to learn." And things like that.

I wrote so serenely about the conditions I saw about me and the needs of the women who worked, that they got a sort of impression all the time that I was like a Settlement Worker, living arbitrarily in certain conditions, and studying them. Well I was, in a way, but I was practising just the same.

Long before that first year was up I had some practical inside knowledge of nine trades, and a week-to-week trial of a dozen more. I had been a waitress in a cheap restaurant, a chambermaid in a hotel, a salesperson, a cap-maker, a necktie maker, a skirt worker, a box-maker, a typist and stenographer, and a nurse—besides a lot of mere investigating experiments.

Next was the job with the actor.

This took a little time, but I worked it. I helped a tired property-woman for nothing; I was willing to lend a hand while I waited to see this one or that one, put a little advertisement in the paper, well worded. "Wages moderate," it said at the end, and I got a place presently.

This was a new kind of life altogether. I had prepared myself as if for imprisonment at hard labor. My theory is that a large part of the complaints people make are due to a lack of preparation. They complain of what they surely ought to have expected, which is foolish. I made up my mind to loss of sleep, to a bad-tempered, tired out, excitable, capricious mistress, and to dear knows what of possible risks among the unprincipled and adventurous.

And I found out right then and there what I half knew before—that people are just *people,* wherever you find them.

As for "improper advances," I met more of that risk as a lady's maid in "the first families" than I did from "the profession."

My mistress was a sweet, weary little woman, supporting a large family of relatives who disapproved of her, and carrying a broken heart well hidden. She was a good actor, too; knew her work well, and from her and the others I was thrown with, I picked up all I wanted to know.

I had no stage ambitions. The acting I meant to do was in a far larger theater and among more exciting scenes. The same old simple tactics of self-restraint and interest in other people, with an unofficious helpfulness, made friends as always, and I started another notebook on this field of study.

I didn't tell the folks at home about this job at all. They had not had definite news of my form of employment since I was in the Settlement nursery. They did not know that I was nursemaid as Mary Harrison, and lady's maid as Ella Meade. It was good practice to change names, takes a lot of active memorizing. I tried it in these simple easy positions, where you are called by name all the time—it might come in handy later on.

And it was not lying either. It is perfectly legal to change your name as often as you want to. Anybody can. I simply took that name for the time being, because I wanted it.

The theater time was immensely interesting. My actor got quite attached to me—said I rested her. I suppose an unemotional restrained temperament is a rest to the other kind.

I had a chance to watch them all, to see how they wore their costumes and changed them, and I helped the makeup man now and then a little, and made friends with him, got him to show me how he did it. He was quite an artist in his line, but it wasn't exactly the line I wanted. The young men had to take old man parts of course, and did, but when the young women had to act old ones they hated it, and tried not to.

I joked with him about it, said he couldn't make a woman look really old; I dared him to try. He said he could make me look ninety—but that I'd never forgive him.

"Oh, ninety!" I said. "That's just caricature. But could you make me look thirty, forty, fifty?"

He looked at me narrowly, sizing up my present age. As far as I could I was trying to seem near thirty, but he knew better.

"You're nothing but a kid," he said, "but I can make you look thirty, forty, *and* fifty—and take your picture into the bargain."

There was a slow rehearsal going on, and I was waiting for my mistress, so I said "Go ahead!"

He had a little camera of his own, and snapped me on the spot—a particular spot; then he sat me down and did my face awhile, and snapped it, putting me in the same place. "Look while it's there," he said. "Old age is coming upon you."

I looked carefully, noting what he had done. I was a quiet, resourceful woman, all of thirty.

Next he turned me into forty, with a few lines and shadows, a "sadder and wiser" sort of face; and then fifty—unmistakably fifty, explaining as he did it the particular wrinkles and saggy places that made the trick.

"Are you scared yet?" he demanded. "Will you be really old?"

"Go ahead!" I ordered gleefully. "This is a great experience." And he put on the years, and took photographs of them, until even I was horrified at the crone he turned out at last.

"Of course you'd have to dress for it," he said, with all an artist's enthusiasm. "George! You're the first woman I've ever seen that would stand for it."

I begged to take the film and have some developed at once, but had to confess to him that I was so unfortunate as to spoil it. That I had the prints made first, enlarged and clear, he did not know.

He was a pleasant man, but became a little too friendly after that, as well as a shade suspicious—said I was a "queer girl."

Anyway, it was time to change again.

CHAPTER TWELVE

In considering all the things that happened in these first stir-ring years of my life, and examining the separate bits of biography I was always preparing—I have pieced together some of them in this account—I see how absurd it is for novelists to try to "end" a story. There is no end to anybody's story, until they are dead, and some people think that is only the beginning.

What I have put together here was written, some of it, when I was very young indeed, when even I admitted I was young. But when I really left home and things began to hap-pen, that is where these close-filled little books pile up. I can, if I want to, make quite a shelf filled full with volumes about My Adventures.

There were those of the first year—good reading too, some of them—fine, fresh, young adventures.

Then there was being called home—that would be a good place to "end" this batch, if I had stayed there. Then there were the things that happened at home, and after I left again, and that Christmas—I guess that'll do. Because that, if it was not an end, was at least a new beginning, a beginning with a most radical change in it.

Things had not stood still at home on account of my absence. It did me good, though not in a gratifying way, to see how well they got on without me. I had put so much effort and earnest thought into getting matters arranged for Mother and Peggy, that I was awfully afraid at first that the clock would stop if I weren't looking. But it did not. I suppose if the things you plant are suitable to the soil and the weather they will grow, whether or no.

That boarder business suited Mother even better than I hoped it would. It was not only that she liked it, but that it strengthened her. I'd really never thought of that side of it much, I was so used to dear Mother's being downtrodden and discouraged.

After all, it wasn't so much Father as an outside force that kept Mother down, it was mostly her ideas of duty. She thought she had to submit and obey and all that; she was bound by her own notions.

There's a lot of philosophy there, I can see. And then there was habit. If you are always being hectored and looked down on, and never have a chance to do anything worthwhile, it does get on your nerves—makes you think you're no good.

And now everything was different. Mother had room to exercise her faculties: that strengthened her. She found she was really earning money. This grew very slowly into her realization. At first she was very timid and frightened by Mrs. Gale's gloomy prognostications. But I could feel the change coming over her, showing in all her letters—the increase of assurance, of hope, of courage.

Then I wrote Peggy and Robert to let up a little on their careful saving of profits, to let Mother feel the business grow under her hand. Soon she began to plan little improvements, to add to the comfort and pleasure of the place, to buy new things. It was just beautiful to me to see her whole outlook widen and brighten and grow firmer, as it were.

Another great help was the society of friends. Dear Mother was very sociable always, but little enough society we ever had when Father was home. He was especially disagreeable to the kind of people she liked best; quite naturally, I suppose, he knew they didn't like him.

But the kind, thoughtful, pleasant women she had about her now, the reliable, cheery, big men, and those boys who simply adored her—well, it worked like a charm.

Best of all was Mary Allen Windsor. That woman is one of the wisest and best I've ever known. She was everything to Mother, and it wasn't a one-sided affair either, for she needed just the kind of loving homeyness that Mother gave her. It was her strong, sound philosophy and the high religious feeling she put into it that had so much effect on Mother's mental attitude, far more than I knew anything about, being away from home.

They sent for me—Peggy did, that is—for two reasons. One was Miss Windsor's illness; she had pneumonia, a long serious affair, and Mother simply would nurse her, business or no business.

Peggy felt the need of help, naturally, and then she had another reason.

I came of course—was glad of an excuse at times. I'd been doing some very disagreeable work—very—and to go back to where there were clean sheets and a bathroom, to say nothing of nice people, was a comfort.

It seemed strange to have sickness in the house. Everybody went on tiptoe. We kept the dining room doors shut and were as quiet as we could be behind them, and all the evening doings were transferred to the Gale house.

It was fortunate for us that it wasn't anything catching; nobody had to leave. But it did need somebody to take hold and help run things, for Mother was heart and soul in that sickroom.

At first I didn't notice anything funny about Peggy, but pretty soon I did. She blew hot and cold at once. She was awfully affectionate when I came, then sort of froze over, and then "melted into tears" at a minute's notice. When I asked her what was the matter, she said, "Oh, nothing," or that she was worried about Mother, or Miss Windsor, or anything that sounded likely. But I knew better. The reason wasn't very far to seek.

It was Robert!

Now I had worried—just the least little bit—about coming back, wondering if he were still of the same mind, and how I should take it if he was. But I needn't have worried even that little.

As to me, I had met several men since I left Robert. One or two of them had been sincerely attracted to me, so I got kind of used to the pressure—I couldn't fall in love with them all, you see. And quite a number had manifested that sort of devotion which makes any cool-headed woman discount the whole lot; it is at once so selfish and so *impersonal.*

It's no compliment—far from it! You being a Female, a Young Unattached Female, and they being Males (of any age, attached or at large), the proper thing is for them to make advances. Also the proper thing for the woman is to make retreats—according to the conventions. In which case they continue to come on.

But I followed different tactics.

I got my first scare in a Chicago workshop—on the stairs leading to it, that is. There were rather dark and narrow stairs and the foreman was coming up as I went down. He took right hold of me and kissed me before I could stop him, but he repented all the way down—back down and head first.

It washed off, all right, and I got another job—didn't go back there, even for my wages. But I was somewhat alarmed as well as angry, and determined to provide against that sort of thing as well as the slower kind.

There was a fine woman doctor I used to see at the Settlement and I went to her.

"Doctor," I said, "I am a young woman, working for my living. I find that some men are disagreeable and some dangerous. Will you give me some very clear advice, both as to the nature and the extent of the danger, and the best methods of self-protection."

She tilted back in her office chair and looked me over. "You are certainly a very cool young woman," she said.

"Why not?" I answered. "If I were traveling in the jungles of Hindustan I'd want to know all about the snakes and tigers; how to avoid them, how to fight them, how to treat injuries. It appears that we women are in another kind of jungle and some of us have never even heard that the cobra is dangerous. I know better than that, but I want to know more. I want some straight, practical knowledge, anatomical and psychological."

"You shall have it," she said. And she gave me books and pamphlets to read—quite a number of them.

I learned a lot. Out of the lot there are two bits of information which ought to prove useful to damsels in distress.

One, for extreme cases, is "the womanly art of self-defense." A woman is not a mouse and a man is not an elephant.

Of course, if one is overwhelmed by numbers, that's another story, or if one is stunned with an unexpected blow. But when just one man tries to "make love" offensively to a woman who doesn't want him to, she need not run, nor shriek, nor faint.

Stand steady, cold, quiet, with a steely eye. If he is not checked by that psychological wall, if he comes too close, kick, kick hard and accurately. This is "unladylike," but not so regrettable as being mishandled.

But there aren't many of those melodramatic episodes. I never had but one, besides that little kiss on the stairs. The real frequent trouble is just impertinence, familiarity and undesired attentions.

And here any woman alive who has the spirit for it may use that so-called "woman's weapon," the tongue. Not to plead, or protest, or scold, but to present, in clear, well-chosen words, the reason of the case.

For instance, a man followed me one night, spoke to me, tried to take my arm. I stopped quite still, under a streetlight, and looked him in the eye.

"Sir," I said, "it is painfully apparent that you have amorous intentions. May I assure you that they are not reciprocated. Will you show your good taste by selecting an object for your attentions who will be more congenial. Good evening."

I went off—alone. He seemed permanently placed under the lamp post, staring.

Being "spoken to" doesn't hurt a woman. Why should not one human being speak to another? Being "insulted" is not an irrecoverable injury. But unless a man is drunk he can hear reason and should be made to.

Well, that's a long digression, but it's what made the difference about Robert. Before I went away he was the First—the Only. And there's no denying that there is a force in first impressions. Now I had seen others. I had seen all kinds of men—young, old, and middle-aged—and that any one of them was "in love" with me was not so startling a fact.

Dear Robert! He was just as nice a man as ever; nicer, in fact, older and wiser and cleverer. And I was just as fond of him as ever, if not more so.

I am yet. He is my brother-in-law.

That is, of course, what I had hoped would happen, but I was pleased to find how honestly glad I was.

Poor little Peggy! She was deeply in love with him. I doubt if she would have been so overwhelmed if it hadn't been for her struggling with it, on my account, bless her heart!

You see, that foolish young man had told her he loved me and she suspected that I had gone away on that account. I don't know how she reasoned it out, but that was her idea, and she had tried to comfort him and be a sister to him and keep the place warm for me to come back to, as it were.

Then he fell in love with her and was ashamed to own it, and she with him, and they were ashamed to own it. And there they were.

It was high time I came home. One night with Peggy, one

good talk with Robert—"Why you blessed children," I said, looking very old and wise, "you dear, heroic, conscientious, noble-hearted geese—just listen to reason, both of you.

"I do not love Robert—hear me swear! Robert does not love me—he needn't swear—he doesn't have to. He's head over ears in love with you, Peggy, and you know it.

"As for your feelings toward him I will not commit myself, but leave you to first find out and then admit."

So I kissed her—and even gave him one, as a Brother Elect—and cleared out.

Peace settled on that part of the household. And a mighty good thing it was; he's been the nicest kind of a husband, and really a son, a good son, to Mother. Also a good brother to me—but then, I have several.

When that was straightened out we just kept things running smoothly and sat around waiting for Miss Windsor to get well.

She did. It took time, but she did. And she and Mother just grew together. There are some women to whom a congenial friendship seems to open a wider range of happiness than even love—that is, the ordinary, average kind of love.

Mother broadened, strengthened, and grew in Mary Allen Windsor's companionship, more than she realized herself; more than any of us realized, until the test came.

They read together books Mother never would have heard of any other way, and talked, discussed things, helped other people to read and discuss. And Miss Windsor seemed so contented and happy with Mother—it was beautiful.

We learned after a while that the man Miss Windsor had loved had died; that is why she was single. And she said she had never expected to be as happy as she was with us.

There we all were, peaceful and contented; Peggy and Robert getting ready to be married some day, and everybody preparing for Christmas.

We were all sitting about in the pleasant parlor one evening—the family, I mean, including Miss Windsor. As it happened the rest of the boarders were all off somewhere or in their rooms, or over in the other house, so it was just us.

Mother had had new curtains put up, lovely ones, and hangings by the folding doors to match. She had bought one or two pictures that she really liked; not works of art, just pictures—colored prints they were, at five dollars apiece, and some photogravures for less—and flowers. The place fairly sang with them.

Peggy, with Robert of course, played softly at the piano, in the shady end of the room. Mother and Miss Windsor and I sat around the big table, each with her favorite magazine.

There was an open fire, another of Mother's luxuries; and the more it blew and snowed outside, the happier we felt.

Then all at once there was a great scuffling and stamping on the steps; the front door opened, letting a fine, cold blast swing our curtains and making the fire flash up—and in walked Father!

There was another man, still stamping in the hall, but that didn't count.

Father! He had come back!

We all started up and stood staring. Mother had her hand to her heart and couldn't seem to speak. Miss Windsor took her other hand and said softly: "Steady, dear." She saw who it was, of course.

"'Tis a fine welcome you are giving me," he said presently, for we were all literally too much astonished to speak.

Then Peggy ran forward and gave him a kiss, and I did, somewhat more slowly, and then Mother. But it was different. I watched her. She had stood there a moment, holding on to her friend's hand; then she had pulled herself together and came to him—sweet, cordial, and so beautiful!

Somehow I had never realized how beautiful Mother was until that night. She was plumper than in her timid, worried days; straighter, so that she looked taller, and her head held like a queen's. She was richly dressed, too—something that I never remembered as a child—gray and rose and silver it was that night, and what with the firelight and the excitement, her face was like a glowing rose.

"You are welcome home, Andrew," she said. "We were startled—not expecting you. But you are welcome." She kissed him, sweetly enough, and turned to the others.

"This is Robert Aylesworth, that I wrote you of, our son-to-be; and this is my friend—my sister—Mary Windsor."

Father was stiffly polite.

"Aye!" he said. "I heard of this son and came to look him over. And I have heard of you, too, Madam." He bowed to her. "I have brought another new relation home with me—come in, laddie."

And there came in from the hall, blushing with shyness, yet bravely cordial, a tall, lean, high-colored young Scotchman.

"Kiss your cousins, my lad!" cried Father, slapping him on the back. "Make him welcome, girls—'tis your own bloodkin, Home MacAvelly, of Homeburn."

Of course we knew there were cousins, Scotch cousins, whole rows and ranks of them, but we had never thought to see one in the flesh. He was good to look on, too, and Mother greeted him like the dear she was.

We got out a jolly little supper for them and sat about talking for a while.

Miss Windsor went to her room and Robert to his; the young cousin was shown another. We girls were sent to bed, and there was no one in the big, bright parlor by the red fire but Mother and Father.

I couldn't stand it. I'm a good creeper, and I crept downstairs again—the back stairs—and in through the kitchen and dining room to the closed parlor doors. A table knife wedged them open softly and the fine new hangings were a further shield.

I wasn't going to have my lifework upset, maybe, and not know about it.

Father was looking well; older, a bit grayer, and thin—his Scotch diet was not so rich as ours, maybe, and perhaps his prolonged stay in other peoples' homes had made him somewhat more appreciative of this one.

Also I fancy he was a trifle awed by the new Something about Mother—not only her air of prosperity and beauty, but a different mental attitude. She was no longer merely something of *his*, she was her own.

But he gathered himself together and began to lay down the law. Doubtless he had rehearsed it to himself many times on the voyage over, or in those cold stone-built chambers on the other side.

He had come back now; he saw his way to making a good living (Father always saw his way, but seldom got to it), and all this boardinghouse experiment must stop at once.

Did he like Robert? Mother asked.

Oh, aye—the lad was well enough. Girls must marry; they would soon be left to themselves and they'd need less money to live on. But he was here now—in his own home—and all this boardinghouse business must stop.

I knew it. It was just what I had been afraid of. Oh, how did he get back?

Then Mother spoke. I could see the pink curve of her cheek, and her fine, shapely hand lying quietly on the arm of her chair.

"Andrew," she said, "I am glad that you bring the matter up at once, so that we have a clear understanding to begin with. I enjoy keeping boarders. I find it a successful and fairly lucrative business and I intend to keep on with it."

He blustered. Somehow the ground was new; he could not drop into his old, superior tone at once. He spoke of the rights of a man in his own house.

"You forget, Andrew," she answered mildly, "that the house is mine. It is perfectly legal and proper for me to run this business if I choose—and I do choose."

He talked of her duty to him.

"I have done my duty to you, as I saw it, for many a long year; I have loved and served you and submitted to all your opinions. Now I shall still love you. You are my husband and the father of my children, but I have opinions of my own now, Andrew. I think that this is right to do—and I shall do it."

It wasn't easy for her, and yet, to my astonishment, it

wasn't half as hard as I should have thought. I suppose if she had stood up to him like that in the beginning things never would have been so hard.

"Let us not quarrel on the night of your homecoming, Andrew," she said in that dear, gentle voice of hers. "You are my loved husband and I am your wife. But you come home to a somewhat different woman from the poor thing you left. I truly think, my dear, that you will be happier with me now than you were then."

And that is precisely what happened.

Father had a room to himself—the big one next to Mother's—and could be grouchy in there by his own little fire if he wanted to. He grew to respect Mary Windsor, even to like her in a way. The boarders kept him in table manners, and, anyway, he wasn't half so arrogant as he had been. Too much home life is not good for some temperaments.

He played chess and checkers evenings, and discussed, endlessly, with those who liked it, inviting chosen ones up to his room for the purpose.

And he seemed to be proud of Mother, to look at her as if she were someone to be considered on her own merits—not merely his wife.

But that night it was rather overwhelming.

I crept upstairs again after a while, quite content and happy. It was good, after all, to have Father back—so long as Mother was able to stand it better.

I walked softly up and down my room and thought it all over.

Mother was safe—safe and happy.

Peggy was going to have an extremely nice husband.

Everything was all right and seemed likely to stay so.

And then I began to think about that new cousin. What a nice name—Home. I'd read about the Homes in Scotch history and knew we were connected.

He was just the type of man I liked: tall, sinewy, active

but quiet, able to sit still or to jump quick—and far.

He had nice eyes, steady, keen, gray-blue eyes that looked right into one. Good, thick, sturdy hair—red-brown, vigorous, fine hair.

Home MacAvelly!

All at once I stopped still in my tracks, and stood, seized by an idea—MacAvelly! His name was MacAvelly, too! And I had thought I never could keep it.

Printed November 1993.
Cover design by Joan Blake.
Text designed and set in Sabon
by Words Worth of Santa Barbara.